THE MALL RAT

By G.B. Mann

PublishAmerica
Baltimore

© 2009 by G.B. Mann.
All rights reserved. No part of this book may be reproduced, stored in a retrieval system or transmitted in any form or by any means without the prior written permission of the publishers, except by a reviewer who may quote brief passages in a review to be printed in a newspaper, magazine or journal.

First printing

All characters in this book are fictitious, and any resemblance to real persons, living or dead, is coincidental.

PublishAmerica has allowed this work to remain exactly as the author intended, verbatim, without editorial input.

ISBN: 978-1-61582-069-6
PUBLISHED BY PUBLISHAMERICA, LLLP
www.publishamerica.com
Baltimore

Printed in the United States of America

*To Sandi, B.J., Heather
and especially Shirley,
Thanks for all your help!*

Table of Contents

To the Reader	7
Welcome to the Jungle	9
Code Purple	14
"My Tummy Hurts"	21
The Fox Guarding the Chicken Coop	25
Chocolate Muffins	29
The Cross Dresser	33
Rob's Last Day	38
The Weatherman	43
More than I Needed to Know	48
Mr. D.I.Y.	51
The Coffee Fag	61
50 Ways to Ask for Water	64
The Best Night Ever	67
A Day in the Life of Devin	74
The Drool King	82
Stalkers	85
How Did I Get Here?	99
The Good Samaritan	105
Color Blind	108
Who Ya Gonna Call?	115
The Stoner Nation	130
Nice Recovery	134
Fani California	140
A Christmas Carol	144
A Christmas Peril	148
And in this Corner…	155
Hitler Youth	159
The Handyman	165
Bono	168
The Garden of Eden	176
It Took Four Years	185
Who's Your Daddy	188

How's the Clam Chowder? 193
I Let Him Do It 198
I Gotta See This 202
Deepthroat 208
Interlude 213
Circle the Wagons 215
Deathrow 220
An Early Christmas Present 231
The Last Rites 237
A Month of Sundays 246
Swan Song 250

To the Reader

"How did we put up with it for so long?"
"I dunno, man, I dunno."

Lyle and I are returning to our table in a bar. We'd just finished talking to a girl we knew at the mall.
It had been a few months since we'd been evicted from the mall, and we were having a catch-up session.
Lyle was my employee, there longer than I owned the place!
The place in question was a seafood stall in a food court in a 200 store mall.

There were no shortage of stories that night or at any of the rehashings.
This book was born out of that mental process. A sifting of so many funny people and circumstances.

I spent ten hours a day there for over five years!
That's a full two years of my life in two rooms. One room a year.
Like a sentence in a prison. Or asylum.
362 sq. Ft.
362 very star-crossed feet!

There was never a dull moment. In 2000 days, the uneventful ones were less than 10%. Continuous action.

Strange customers. Ghosts. Floods. You name it.

Ultimately this is a story of business failure, but not based on market forces.

I've changed the names to protect the guilty, so to speak. I have no personal issue with these people I write about. In many cases I don't even know them.

Even though I saw some pretty horrible interpersonal behavior, I don't hold grudges. People are people are funny.

Only the events and facts are important.

These are just people in a moment of their lives. Probably an unfortunate one. But a comical one.

In many cases they were unaware someone was taking all of this in.

But I was. I'm the Mall Rat. Say Cheese.

Gary B. Mann
St. Patrick's Day 2009

Welcome to the Jungle

It's training time.
This really sucks.
I'm having a smoke in the company parking lot.
It's snowing.
But it's spring, and the snow is now melting on contact.
A real ho-hum day.
To go along with my ho-hum "training."
I'm all revved up for my new venture, the deep-fried seafood kiosk in the mall.
Only this "training" is absolutely useless.
It's a 3 digit chain, so I'm not exactly at University of McDonald's!
"So, how is this combo put together?"
"You're in a mall. It's different."
"How does this POS system work?"
"You have the old kind. Don't worry about it."
I hate making coleslaw.
I imagine being in a salt mine in Russia with Solzhenitsyn.
"Don't worry. In the mall slaw doesn't come with the meals. You use different equipment."

Great. I was free labor.

Finally, I get a great description of how the chicken rotisserie system works.

Turns out the kiosks don't sell chicken!

I'm not making this up!

I'm at Uncle Bingo's School of Fish!

Finally, I "graduate."

Wow, what a diploma! It'll end up in the basement with the others. In my "memories" box.

I'm now qualified to cook fish.

My 9th designation on this planet!

In reality, I can't even use a can opener!

On "Graduation Day," the staff at this training center/restaurant all have the same look on their faces.

"I know, I didn't help you at all. Good luck."

It actually made me laugh, as they had the whole training "routine" down to an art.

So, armed with all this new-found knowledge of the fast food industry, I plunged into my new home at the mall.

And home it would be!

It's fast food. In a mall. You serve hundreds, tens of thousands walk by. Ten to fourteen hours a day.

The people who sold me the business were of little help either.

They were desperate to get out and they could only mouth, "Yul-learn," to any inquiry I had about my recently purchased business.

But the price was low.

It had to be.

The company books were a creative fantasy, and on a couple of lean days my bowels barely made it home!

It probably lost a few dollars in reality. But this place was so out of whack that basing anything on what I got from them was a mistake. Why bother?

Take what you got and build.

Location's pretty good.

Got 3,000 customers a month. Need 6,000. Double.

And the staff?
The staff!
Lyle, Rob and Nat.
Lyle will be there till the bitter end.

A really good kid. My confidante. Assistant Manager. Great cook. Eighteen at the time. Baby face.

Someone who can be trusted and take care of things. Act in our best interests. Responsible.

Nat's an easygoing kid. Huge druggie! He was apparently so wasted on some drug that our company logo was talking to him. During a shift! Nice kid, though.

And Rob.

One could write a book on Rob. A real 21st century youth. He was so depressed by it all that at the end he was I.D.-ing seniors on Senior's Day!

I learn everything from these 3. They're all competent, to some degree. It's 3 eighteen-year olds and me! Need I say more!

I never really ever got good at cooking. I was pretty good with the customers, but in the kitchen I was more in the way, than doing way more!

I gradually got into the swing of things. It was a 100% learning curve. And the whole drama of the mall started to unfold.

A mini community, with an ever-changing cast. A couple of thousand workers here, a few dropping off, new ones all the time.

I didn't realize I actually interact with some of these people, know things about their lives. Friends, enemies, romantic angles, criminal minds, everything.

I thought it was just a matter of running a business. Figure out the four or five components of this operation and it'll be smooth sailing!

And it was.

Except it was kind of like doing it next to some huge mental institution. Mixing patients into the public at large. Escapees!

One kind of public I met in the first week or two was my first stalker.
"The Original Butterface."
She flew over the counter at me. The boys jeered her off.

The boys branded her a "butterface." (Everything is good, but-her-face.) This was due to one slightly crooked tooth. She eventually got braces.

I quickly realized that the boys had very suspect taste in women. This girl had the body of a beer poster girl.

Like a homing pigeon, she showed up on our second last day! She didn't know we were going out. From one end to the other. She was there.

And to welcome me to the mall I got a nice visit from the mall Manager and the Marketing Lady. He's cordial. I sense his harmlessness. This guy will never take much interest in the mall. This whole place is on auto-pilot to him.

And that's good. Disinterested types are easy to get along with, and never give you too much trouble.

The Marketing Lady is another story. She's glaring at me. Through me. This person really doesn't like me. She's demented.

What gives?

Well, Mr. Manager probably has golf and a family.

This woman has this job. And nothing else.

She's about my age. No husband. No kids. Getting a little bitter about her lot in life. Thinks it should have been better.

And this bitterness manifests itself in all aspects of one's life.

Like this job!

I'm too young to own this, in your eyes. I have a huge castle on a hill with a perfect family. We all smile perfectly as we play in the sand on the beach. The beach is on the hill! Yeesh, the vibe off this woman is really uncomfortable.

I must have known her in a former life.

Let's see…I was some kind of feudal landlord who oppressed her family and starved them to death. I lived in luxury as her low-breed brethren toiled the fields. I looked at them with disgust as I rode past their ilk in my horse-drawn carriage.

Or something.

But now somehow I, the victim, have done something to them! I must press some button in them that highlights the inadequacy of their lives. Their miserable lives. I'm a raw nerve.

People like this suck!

But I only have to endure these 2 for a couple of minutes. It's all small-talk with a dash of hate.

THE MALL RAT

Mr. Manager will eventually get fired for letting maintenance and trades people steal equipment from the mall!

My initial read on the Marketing Lady will be prophetic!

Remember her. I do. In a comical way. And so these were my original cast. The "Good Ship Billy's" was off and running! Storm clouds up ahead!

Code Purple

Not that it really mattered, but sometimes you totally misjudge someone.
What you see ain't what you get! Judging the book by the cover, so to speak.

I would have hired Reg anyway. He worked here before and knew the ropes. No time to train people. I did the most remarkable recycling job of the "previous employees."

Reg with his high school football jacket. Always a girl in tow. Super polite. Looked like he was college bound.

That was my perception!

Same high school as Lyle. Lyle worked with him before. Said he was useless. And "weird."

What's "weird?" Everyone's "weird" these days, they even work at it!

Lyle's nickname for Reg doesn't sound too hopeful—referring to his head as being made of a substance no one likes to step in!

He can't be that bad!

But he is. I'd never seen "white fries" before, fried for all of 1 minute!

Lousy attitude too. Constant war with his parents—he not wanting to do much after high school—they wanting him to go to the University of Very

Far Away. In the end, he'd flunk out of technical school and force his parents to buy him a car and condo so he could work in a warehouse!

What was Reg's problem?
He didn't smoke. Or do drugs. He drank at normal pace for a young guy, and was a funny kind of drunk.
None of the above.
Reg's problem was the Internet!
Porn-Hate web sites. Gothic stuff.
Messages-Harassing women. Games. No holds barred.
And apparently he was very good at computers.
One evening, I went to the back room to find Reg with his laptop on the prep table.
This is work?
OK. Do your schoolwork. Pass your courses. We're not busy.
Hmm. This is a rather interesting "course."
It appears to be a rather promiscuous naked woman pulling what looks to be these noticeable large black balls from her nether regions! Strung together.
From the size of them I can deduct that they were "previously" under quite a bit of pressure!
Reg informs me that we are now bonding.
Hmm. That's interesting.

I didn't stick around long, and Reg probably went on to some Rammstein videos.
This is Reg.

Lyle always would tell me funny stories from yesteryear about how dumb and weird Reg was. Reg was ADD itself.
But one day I had a story for Lyle.
Having a smoke one day, a new girl in the mall strikes up a conversation with me.
"I know one of your employees."
"Oh yeah, who?"
"Reg."

I tried to remain cool, but my mind was already thinking about how he knew this girl, and how negative it could be.

"Yeah, he went out with my sister. After they broke up, he started a hate website on her. We had the state police look into it, but he left no trace."

I was shocked!

She provided some more details. Her father was in some army for 20 years and wanted to kill Reg. They had some kind of restraining order on him.

Whew, I saw hate.

I changed the subject, finished my cigarette. And left.

Holly smokes, Reg is a real sicko.

If this story is true. Who knows?

It's the kind of story I'll tell Lyle, and no one else. Knowledge is power, so I usually tell no one of what I see and hear. It's a good policy.

Only one way to see if this is true, so I wait until Reg and I are working one night and ease him into it.

By the look on his face, he's guilty as charged!

His defence is that he got away with it! Now time to gloat. He says he totally took advantage of her, even did the deed on the sister's bed! The one defending her!

I immediately see a source of future strife, if properly nurtured, and press for details on the sister's bedroom! A lever. A wedge.

Interesting. And my girl doesn't even know it! She'd totally blow!

Reg tells me he's "reformed."

Fat chance. He's probably worse.

As I get to know her, I can really sense her anger. Never stated, just underlying. I do tell Lyle. He's shocked but not overly surprised. I told you so.

This girl is a full time mall worker, Reg is part-time—if I can confine him to nights and weekends, their paths won't cross. If I can help it. If I see her coming, I kick Reg to the back. It'll be easy.

But it doesn't work!

And they face each other at my counter. With me there.

Reg is sheepish.

She's right in his face, calling him all sorts of things.

And she comes back for more, from time to time. And each time gets more in his face, and starts to press him on things. She's very indignant. Indignant versus "crawl under a rock" is pathetic!

Reg is pathetic—No question about it.

Time to throw some gas on the fire! Help Reg out.

You want it to end?

"Next time, tell her about your escapades in her bedroom! Include a few details as only she would know, and she'll flip."

Reg is instantly sold on this idea. No questions asked!

Here she comes again…

And he does it! And includes the fate of some pillowcase or something! Thar' she blows! She never saw it coming. Furious. Enraged.

He's won.

She storms off and never mentions this around me again. No more counter visits. Acts like none of it happened!

I won't forget the look on Reg's face as I told him (after the fact, ha, ha) about how much discord "he'd" just created between the sisters. Defending her sweet innocent little sister, while little sis is using her bed and bedding for Reg the Ripper's nefarious designs! This is your checkmate, Reg, don't you get it? Actually, I personally detest Reg's actions, but can't stand by and see a fellow male looking so weak!

I guess you could say from this point I harbored no illusions about Reg!

People like this always bring you trouble. This was just one chapter of Reg's life. Probably only a small one.

He was a mess. And a lousy worker. With a lousy attitude.

Reg's attitude would manifest itself in some strange ways.

Doing meaningless, counter-productive tasks, for example.

Like filling the drain in the closet with cement!

Or "cleaning." This would consist of throwing out all kinds of useful things we needed.

Reg would come up with some real zingers, usually implemented when I wasn't around.

And he gave us the best "Code Purple" of all time.

A Code Purple is very simple: It's the color of Lyle's face when I return from a break or trip and some major screw-up has happened.

Grease Trap Overflow? Code Purple.

Hot Table burned dry? Code Purple.

Major Customer Trouble? Code Purple.

So what could Reg do to create the ultimate "Code Purple?"

A bio-hazard? Mug Santa? No, No—Simplicity. The biggest idiots are the simplest ones.

I'll give you a hint—How many Reg's does it take to…?

If you answered, "Change a Lightbulb," you would have answered correctly!

All you know about Reg has now prepared you for the ultimate piece of stupidity—Changing Lightbulbs.

In the backroom, there are 4 sets of 2 tube lights—8 total.

If 4 or 5 work, it's great.

Nightclub effect. Our lounge.

If we know of an upcoming inspection, we may pull a Potemkin and go for 6 or 7, then take the lights out after.

So I go for my break. A couple of hours. A couple of hours!

I return. Go in "the customer way," through the food court, to the counter.

It's definitely a "Code Purple!!!!!"

"You won't believe it!"

No, I probably won't, but try me.

"Reg electrocuted himself"

"What?" (I'm picturing a minor finger near some electricity kind of thing.)

"Come Around."

I walk around and enter the back door. Lyle is purple. Deep purple. He's in shock. But Reg looks like he just survived a natural disaster!

White—Hair messed up. Sitting down. Giddy. Hands on Knees.
Moaning. The moaning was very funny!
They look and point up.
Our genius decided he was going to "change lightbulbs."
Never mind we had no replacements!

Reg decided to play "Musical Lightbulbs."
He stood on a milk crate and stuck his fingers where they didn't belong until he took the full force of our power supply!
According to Lyle, at the moment of impact everything went dead for a second or two—the fryers, cash register, lights, everything!

Reg was taking it all, and the milk crates saved his life, according to the mall electrician I asked as he inspected "Thomas Alva's" handiwork.
Lucky man.
We didn't bother calling an ambulance!
This was like a home-perm gone wrong, except it was a home-electroshock treatment. They're about the same, really.
From the amount of blood in Lyle's face and neck, it probably would have been him in the ambulance anyway!

Reg eventually left my employ.
It was a joyous day, and my elation was apparent for all to see.
He actually fired himself. Of course.
Before going on a long trip to Europe with his family, he told me our place wasn't full-time enough for him, and that upon return he'd be working elsewhere.
I quickly took him at his word, and wished him a great holiday and success in whatever was next. You were great. Bye Bye.
He actually phoned another employee when he came back to see if he "still had a job."
I looked mystified. "No."

He eventually ended up in a warehouse of a well-known toy retailer. He can't do too much damage there. Ah, yes he can.
His real plan was to work for the security company that handles the mall's security!

To serve and protect?

Hardly.

He wanted to stalk women in the parking lots armed with hand cuffs and a uniform!

He was serious, and mentioned a girl or two. Knew their cars. Schedules. Frequented their stores to be chummy. And gain trust.

Don't worry. While he was away, I phoned the security company manager, and he never got hired.

But that's another story.

"My Tummy Hurts"

The world we live in today is vastly different from a generation or two ago.

Think of the difference in the amount of food consumed at home versus outside. And made by someone else.

When I was a kid, getting a bucket of Kentucky Fried twice a year was a big deal!

Today, every conceivable food idea is franchised.

That's how much we eat out.

And part of that change is the amount of control we surrender to others' sanitation and preparation standards!

Take it from someone who has been in the "back" of many a food stall, the people who work in these places are, by and large, appalling.

And they cook your food.

They wipe their noses. Don't wash their hands.

They touch dirty things. No soap and water.

They use the bathroom. Forget it.

That person in front of you has something to do with what will be in your stomach very soon!

It's a couple of years into my lease. Business is pretty good. Food courts work on rankings. We've constantly moved up and improved. The seas of customers are there. It's your job to build the first-timers, who become regulars, who become your business.

But a new place is opening up. The mall has managed to salvage 350 sq. ft. of space. So, the 14th entry in the race will be a southern Cajun-style chicken place. Only it's a "turkey."

It's taking forever to get this place ready. They're spending a fortune. A few months after opening they'll try to start unloading, oops, I mean, selling it.

And the public doesn't realize how crazy business gets. Tens of thousands just for tiles. Signs are usually locally custom-made, so you have no idea how much neon and styrofoam can cost. Pick an outrageous estimate, then double it. At least.

Finally, Opening Day comes.

Actually I was amazed!

They totally blew the direct competition out of the water. The Chinese place had literally 10 customers. A normal Saturday they'd serve 200.

Everyone was trying it.

And they put a slight dent in other places as well. I saw a few of my regulars there.

This lasted for a week or two, then it became more settled and regular. The market for chow mein came back!

I'm always interested in whatever's going on around me, so out of curiosity I'd ask customers who I'd seen eating there. Or perhaps "the new place" would come up in conversation with people waiting for our fish.

THE MALL RAT

And I noticed a trend. To a person, they all said it made them sick. Mildly to violently!

I put this down to the fact the chicken was pre-cooked and served cafeteria-style. Or maybe they just weren't following some important, yet neglected, prep function.

Who knows?

Who cares?

As long as they weren't very good at this, they were of no threat to me!

Chinese cooking Cajun, Koreans make tacos.

Live and let live. Or die.

One of their cooks was an old guy who worked at the Chinese place. Moonlighting at nights, he seemed to like it there better than the gross kitchen on the other side of the court.

If you have no customers, the only way you'll get some is by standing there. Sales is a waiting game, unfortunately!

And it's a weekday night. Not a lot of customers, but I'll stand here and keep watch for awhile.

Time for the old guy's break over at chicken land.

He's walking toward me.

He stops.

He puts his finger up his nose.

And he pulls out the biggest snot you've ever seen!!!!!

At 15 feet I can identify "parts" of this snot.

It's LONG and STRINGY and NASTY.

And then he EATS it!

Ugh!

He doesn't flick it on the floor. He doesn't take out a tissue. Zero.

He eats it!

Strangely, I don't think he even noticed me, he was that focused on "the pick of the day."

I always knew this old guy was really dirty. But not this dirty!

He then proceeded to the washroom and went back to work. I'm not sure he washed his hands.
Chicken glazed in mucus and God knows what else.

I always laugh when I think of that customer with the grimace on his face describing his wife's 3am trip to the "throne of repentance." His contorted face! "That chicken was bad."
So be careful where you eat. I now consciously increase the amount of food I prepare myself.
One day the chicken place was in darkness at 9:20. They were serving someone at 9:33!
Caveat Emptor.
No. No. Bon Appétit!

So the next time you feel a little queasy…

The Fox Guarding the Chicken Coop

Every once in awhile you meet someone who truly mystifies you. A person whose actions you just can't explain. On any level.
Jeff was such a person.
Dumb and Dumber all in one.
Somehow, these people make it through. I figure it's "God's Great Gift" that somehow, no matter how dumb, even the most brain-dead clump can somehow bumble through three score and ten.

Such a person was Jeff.
Jeff was a mall security guard. Security guards come in two varieties: over-zealous cop-wannabes, and lethargic drupe-a-long's who can barely fill out Inspection Sheets.

Jeff was the latter, although he could show signs of a power-trip once in awhile.

Jeff bought our food because we gave him a "mall staff discount." He was a real cheapskate, and had one of those personalities that just rubbed you the wrong way. The challenging look of a little person! And he'd always have something dumb to say. So if you added it up, we didn't want to know Jeff.

But he was usually around. And we soon find out that he's a gymnast. He's a little shrimp. I can see it. Wow. Important information. Flush!

Like I say, he's always babbling on with some unimportant conversation line, and he's following up the gymnast stuff by telling us he could actually scale up to our ceiling, crawl through whatever's up there, and get down on the other side, in the back room.

The employees all have a look at it, and give their various opinions on whether it would be possible. You'd have to be pretty light or the ceiling would collapse.

How many meaningless conversations have I ever had!

So, you can swing through a ceiling. We haven't been primates for a few thousand years, so your "skill" doesn't mean much to me. Join the circus.

What I don't realize is that this guy was describing a crime he was going to commit. Partially, anyway. "If I Did It" became, "This Is How Someone Else Would Do It."

Criminals, successful ones anyway, are highly intelligent people who you never hear of simply because they commit the crime in a foolproof manner, and vanish. No apparent connection. Zero. They vanish.

Jeff didn't get this.

Since the staff had generally agreed that it would be next to impossible to get through the ceiling, it somehow triggered the idea in Jeff's brain to use this as the cover for a break-in! Or something.

Don't even try to figure Jeff out.

It's 3am—I'm sleeping.
The phone rings.
"This is mall security, there's been a break-in at your place. Come right over."

I go to the mall.
The officer on the scene?

Jeff.
Method of entry?
The ceiling.
All the contents of the freezer are everywhere.

Evidently, Jeff, oops, I mean the thief, thought we kept money in the freezer. "Cold hard cash."

This is crap.

There's too much wrong with this crime scene. First and foremost, how did Jeff, oops, I mean the thief, manage to jump and miss all kinds of boxes of cups, lids, and things? Things that make huge messes.

No, no. All these boxes were stacked neatly on the table.

Jeff's nervous, but he doesn't feel guilty because he didn't get anything. That's the truth.

He's waiting inside Billy's when I get there, so his fingerprints are everywhere and you won't find any up in the ceiling, if you were dumb enough to look. Only on the tiles. Jeff will say he went up there to look for the thief!

I don't even phone the police.

No point. Jeff had a key for every lock in the building.

I put all the stuff back in the freezer and go home.

The next day all the staff point the finger at Jeff. Lyle's right.

Our only other suspect is a kid who tried out for a job some time ago. He was really funny.

My staff would tell me the whole time he was there he just kept asking them where we kept the money, or odd questions about money handling procedures. Always trying to find the weak link!

I fired him when I rounded the corner and saw a latex glove submerging into the fryer, like the last 2 seconds of the Titanic. I didn't even ask him how he did it, because he was going at the end of the shift anyway.

We also concluded that he wasn't smart enough to break-in.

But we can't do much about it.

Until Jeff strikes again!

No gain, no guilt. If at first you don't succeed…

He now starts stealing bottled drinks from our unlocked coolers in the front. At night.

I'm informed of this by a cleaner who happens to be working late one night.

Too bad, Jeff, this cleaner doesn't like you much, and now intends to phone the security company!

And he does.

And Jeff gets in trouble.

But Jeff is a fast thinker. He tells the boss that I, yes I, gave him permission to take drinks at night!

What?

So the boss gives Jeff an ultimatum:

Get a letter from Billy's Owner saying he gave you this permission, or be fired!

Jeff appears. He's actually stupid enough to ask me to go along with this?

I laugh in Jeff's face. You've got to be joking. Why would anyone do that? I phone the boss and tell him you can't pay money for security, and then have the security rip you off. It's the fox guarding the chicken coop. What part of "security" don't you get? So Jeff's fired.

(I'm amazed it took this much! The security company sounds none too "reliable"!)

Jeff pulled an OJ. It's better to walk before they make you run, dummy! If you get away with something, call it a day. Consider yourself lucky. Don't push it. Get caught at something else, and pay the price anyway!

Duh.

Somehow, people like Jeff make it through this world. Dumb and Dumber, all in one. God's Great Gift to the world. Keep him next time.

Chocolate Muffins

I really don't know how I missed out on this one.
I only vacated my post to go to the back for less than half a minute.
In that half minute, I missed out on a lot!

It's Sunday.
Have I ever mentioned how much I despise Sundays?
My misery is compounded by the fact that I'm working with the world's most depressed teenager, Brian.
He's always down.
There's no need to do anything, because he's a "the-end-of—the-world-is-near" kind of guy.
Depression is rampant in our society. It's tangible off Brian. He exudes negativity.
The customers are endearingly referred to as "soul suckers."
"Why cook the food properly when these soul suckers will eventually die," kind of guy.

I'll only ever see him excited twice.
He can actually smile.

One time will be today.

The other time was when the ghost tossed a C.D. off a shelf while he was eating. That got his attention.

The C.D. went right over his little old depressed head.

But it got his attention and pumped some life into his corpse-in-waiting.

So I'm here on Sunday with Mr. Exciting.

He drags his ass all day like he's doing a menial task in Detention.

So I'm off to the back to get something.

I have to work hard on Sundays because I always have my weakest employees working then.

It makes me laugh when I think of the idiots I've had cooking on Sundays.

There's some fine talents there. One guy cooked four calamari orders that came out looking like four bowling balls!

I asked him if he would have eaten any of his creations. "Two of them."

So today's Stooge is Brian.

I'm doing two people's jobs here.

I've grabbed whatever it was and I'm returning to my cash register.

What's that?

I look.

I look again.

How could anyone trip and drop a tray of what looks to be those huge muffins you get at supermarket superstores? What a waste.

"Looks like crap," says the Despondent One.

Holy crap, it is crap!

In my absence, someone has dropped four or five bombs on the floor in front of the next kiosk!!!!!!!!

In a walking lane!

The people in the next kiosk aren't acting unusual, so now I'm wondering how someone could pull this off. Or why?

Houdini couldn't do this. Not that he'd want to.

Five large globs of fecal matter.

In descending sizes, like a family.

Like all people with immature, juvenile minds, Brian and I are finding this very funny.

Convulsively funny.

Shorts or long trousers?

We go with shorts. (We are assuming it's a man. No woman would do this!)

Were they walking to or from the bathrooms, thirty feet away?

Hard to know. This kind of creature may be hard to understand!

And then some dough-head steps in one of the globs!

A few prints leading away from the scene.

We find this funny.

And a lot of passers-by are screwing up their faces and pointing at the lumps of crap.

Of course we find this funny as well.

I've never seen Brian so happy!

My ribs are hurting.

So are Brian's.

My imitations of all of this just keep us laughing.

Tears are forming in Brian's eyes.

And because our mall is so "crappy," the clean-up crew takes forever to arrive.

When "Homeland Security" arrives, the looks on their faces set us off again.

This deal just keeps on giving!

They are repulsed beyond all!

One of them bolts immediately, sending us into doubled-over fits of laughter.

This is too much.

The rest of them go through some kind of Philippino decision-making process to arrive at who will do what.

They approach the globs like they're toxic.

Laughing this much is actually draining!

One of those old ladies looks so angry.

Of course this makes us laugh more.

Finally, the show is over.
All the Philippinos are talking to themselves.
For one brief moment Brian was lifted out of his "Casket of Doom."
It took five "chocolate muffins" to do it.
Courtesy of "Who-Dun-It."
And I only left for seconds.
Bravo.
Your artistry humbles us.
But don't call us. And we won't call you.

The Cross Dresser

I loved this guy.
Every once in awhile he'd come around to brighten up your day.
He was mixed up in a harmless way.
He was The Cross Dresser.

I don't understand Cross-Dressing.
"I guess to each his own."
The smell of perfume makes me nauseous.
If I extend my feet to the position necessary to wear heels, my whole leg hurts.
So the whole thing is lost on me.

And this guy is not the most attractive woman either.
He's tall. Too tall.
Irish features.
And he has a give-away bald spot going on.
He's an ugly guy. She's an ugly gal. Either way.
But whatever he sees in the mirror every morning, I don't know.
By the way, he's not a poor cross-dresser. I saw him in the parking lot and at the gas station getting out of a Range Rover!

So he's "pretty" well off. No joke.
And he gets up every morning and puts on his dress and make-up.
And goes to malls. I guess.
He's not exactly a fashionable dresser either. He's a bit of a "Klinger."
And due to his unattractive features the make-up accentuates his "flaws" rather than covers them up. It's a man all right.

I actually sat next to a "Klinger" at Universal Studios, on a ride. Poor guy. Ugly polka dot dress. Body hair problem. And he had all these Oriental tourists laughing at him.
There are some things that you just don't want to think about.
And this guy's one of them.

I guess his sexual orientation is obvious. But I can't see what man would want to be with Dame Edna here.
And you can't attract too many women while dressed as one. Or maybe you can.
Sorry Dame Edna. He's a little more to the Dee Snider side.
In any event, he's a sight for sore eyes.

And he always goes to the washrooms here at the mall.
More stuff I don't want to think about.
What washroom does Twinkle Toes go to?
Three choices.
Men's, Women's, or Family.
To be honest I wouldn't want to be in any of these places when this guy rolls in.
He can't go to the Women's, can he?
The Family? Where's his "Family"?
I guess that leaves the Men's.
Let's rule out the urinals and put him down as a sitter.
Actually, the urinals would be quite funny. I wonder if he wears a thong!?
But he's still in there dressed as an ugly middle-aged woman.
It's not right.
It would be funny if, for a split second, some guy thought he was a woman,

And got all excited.

Then the brain receives the gruesome truth. Or doesn't. Jerry Springer time.

Jerry : You had to know she was a man!

Man : No, Jerry. I didn't.

Who knows?

It's all under the category of "Things I Don't Want to Think About."

And every time he passes by me, if we make eye contact, he has this sheepish, guilty look on his face.

These types lead conflicted lives for sure.

I usually roll my eyes. I can't take him seriously.

My employees love this guy too.

He doesn't come around on a regular basis, so sometimes there'll be someone new to snicker at him.

I once told a customer that the cross-dresser had entered the washroom area and would soon be emerging.

Can you spot him?

It was a gas watching my less-than-nonchalant customer eyeballing everyone.

And one day he actually decided to buy food from us!

Pass by twenty times, and on the twenty-first he decides it's time for Fish-n-Chips.

I have to serve him.

I don't want to.

He speaks.

His "voice" is so funny. He's trying to sound like a deranged auntie.

Sometimes it's hard to keep your composure.

It's even harder when Stan is standing in the cooking area mimicking Aunt Ethel out here.

Shut your mouth Stan, this is hard enough as it is.

This guy knows we know he's a man, so remain cool. We don't want to look like hicks, even though we are.

Having to make eye-contact with this person makes me uneasy.
And that make-up. Garish.
Goodness. He looks like a Raggedy-Ann doll left out in the rain. That rouge is just hideous. He's a bit of a freak in my books.

In any event, I survive.
He goes off to the bathrooms while I chastise Stan and threaten everyone with having to serve Tinkie-Winkie's food to him.
The staff laughs at that.
But I'm serious.
I'm the boss, and I'm going to invoke that card.
"I command you to serve Mr. Marion Cunningham!
They jeer me.
The Fishman. The Boss.
You disloyal swine.

Ok, Twinkle Toes is back.
I try to keep my head.
Back on to him, I'm laughing so hard my ribs are shaking.
To his face, I'm a humble food worker bringing out his fare.
Ten seconds and I'm free.
Put down the tray and wish him a nice day. Over. Thanks for coming.
I've now completed the put-down-the-tray part.
Summon the courage for one more nano-second of eye contact, and some phony end-of-transaction "greeting," and I'm home-free.

"She's got a penis."
"She's got a penis."
Hark! What do I hear?
Could this be Stan doing the unthinkable?
"She's got a penis."
Shut your f****** mouth Stan. Visions of the mall administration and vague Human Rights Groups chasing me with pitchforks enter my head.
If I can hear it, he can too.
What misery.
"She's got a penis."

THE MALL RAT

"Thank you and have a nice day."
His face is stone cold.
Hey, I didn't hear that and neither did you. "Thanks for coming."
He's really pissed.
My only hope is that if he complains to anyone, his credibility won't be too high.
Who am I kidding?
He's the perfect victim.
Let's hope he's publicity-shy.
I turn around to face Stan.
I'm furious.
Then I burst out laughing.
I can't believe how callous Stan is.

And the few times we saw this guy after this, he'd give me a really dirty look. I think we hurt his feelings.

Needless to say, I think we lost a customer!

Rob's Last Day

No chronicle of Billy's would be complete without mention of Rob.
One of the "Originals."
On the first day I owned the place there he was.
Braces and all.
He got jumped over near the station by a bunch of Natives.
They punched his face in, and broke his teeth up.
So now it was reconstructive surgery and braces.

Rob was the typical angry young man. Semi-Gothic. Fashionable Gothic.
He'd complain about everything.
And he just hated the customers.
We'd refer to him as "Customer Service Specialist Rob Smith." Lyle and I.
By the way, his name tag read "Boob."

He was a Boob all right.
I just couldn't figure out what kind of mall had a trash compactor that took an hour to get to and back.
It was actually 2 minutes away when I had time to check it out.

THE MALL RAT

Where did Boob go?

Apparently, this was weed—smoking time, so he would adjourn to the parking lot and walk around.

He wasn't the most inconspicuous type, and one day a security guard appeared to tell me one of my employees was snooping around cars in the parking lot.

I couldn't very well tell him that it's only Rob on a "toke break," so I tell him that Rob is harmless and likes wandering around. This isn't very convincing.

I then tell Rob to stop being such a moron, and try to look like a shopper or something.

Lyle tells me Rob used to kneel down in the cooking area and blow weed smoke up into the hood fan. During operating hours.

The angry young man, flaunting all the rules. I'm "evil," watch out!
One night we had a real bitchy woman.
She was ordering us around like peons.
Not Rob.
I could hear him squashing her take-out box, as she barked another order at us.
Miss High Class strutted away with about 6 pieces of toilet paper attached to one of her heels, courtesy of the mall washrooms.
She looked ridiculously ironic.

And Rob took every opportunity to mess with people.
We ran a Senior's Day, every Tuesday.
Rob would I.D. old people to see if they were old enough to get the discount!
It was totally stupid.
But he insisted these criminal geriatrics had to be dealt with.

For whatever reason, Rob really knew how to cook fish and chips.
All the best food compliments were directed at him.
This was a good high school job, but now Rob had to move out.
And this job would never support rent and a car.
All right if you're in your parents' basement, but not in the real world.

And Rob slowly realized this.
And Billy's started to become a real drag to our angry young man.
Every shift with Rob seemed like an eternity.
You'd do all the work.
And when he left, it was like he was at the prison gates getting out after 15 years!

And one day our luck changed.
Rob told us he was quitting!
Lyle looked like he'd won the lottery!
I quickly calculated how many more hours I'd have to spend with him!
This many more shifts, but less if I manipulate the schedule.
And each shift is a real grind.
They say you are what you really are when you're alone.
Ditto for when you're leaving a job.
You can go out in an obliging, nice way.
Or be a piece of crap.
Rob chooses the crap option.

Finally, I can see the last shift.
It's going to be a Saturday.
I don't want to spend the whole day with him, so I schedule him for 10 to 2, with fellow "A-team" member SlimJim doing the honors from 2 to 8. Six hours of SlimJim. I must be nuts. On a Saturday.

Rob's all smiles today.
I just want the time to go by, so I don't make him do much.
Soon he'll be gone.
No more home improvement projects, Gothic weirdo friends, or outbursts of any kind.
But we're busy.
Very busy.
It's Saturday.
And Rob wants to dog it.
You might as well be dislikeable to the end.
And every order takes 10 minutes or more.

THE MALL RAT

Rob's having a grand old time back there.
He has this "Look at me. See how obnoxious I am" look on his face.

I'll exact my revenge.
He's giving me as a reference for future jobs.
I use this power as my way of getting even with former employees.
I don't return the call for one of his references.
Another one I purposely give an air of insincerity, so the caller thinks I'm hiding something.
I laugh as I put the phone down.
"Who was that?," asks Lyle.
"No one," says a happier former employer.

But I'm stuck with him right now.
And this little act is getting old.
While Rob has this totally stupid look on his face, I have to deal with the growing legion of very annoyed customers.
I'm thinking of all the episodes and BS I've put up with up until now, and hope the next few minutes passes and I can finally see the end of his antics.
If this were a movie, the next scene would be the back door flinging open and me tossing him out by the shirt. "You're no good away." Then I'd spit on the ground.
But right now I'm not in a movie, and reality really sucks.
Somehow it occurs to Rob that he'll be out of here soon, and he can't leave this mess for SlimJim.
So he speeds up.
He's really "doin'er" now.
And then all of a sudden I hear the loudest scream ever! The epicenter is about 8 feet behind me.
Idiot Rob has burned himself!
"AAAhhhhhhhhh." (repeat) (extend).

This is what people like this don't realize. Not only have you been a total jerk all day, you end it by pulling another idiot move. At least you're doing it to yourself. So I kind of think this is funny.

By the way, you can hear this scream in Kentucky.

I'm serious, this ADD-GOTH-teenager can scream louder than anyone you know.
Every single person in the food court is looking at Billy's.
Looking at me.
I turn to see a bottle of Caesar dressing whizzing past, against the wall. How interesting. First Caesar bottle in space.
Rob's so fast I barely see the back of his head.
He storms out the back.
He then yells, "Fxck This," at the top of his lungs.
He already has an audience, so everyone hears this as well.
This is not the kind of corporate image I want to portray.
But I'm the master of nonchalant, so I don't miss a beat.
"Next?"

I'm the only one there for the next 20 minutes.
All I can remember is making the most ridiculous fish sandwich for a take-out order. Sorry.
Strangely enough, it was the only shift where SlimJim came through for me. He actually cooked the right orders fast. Never again.
SlimJim once asked me if Homer Simpson was still alive.

Anyway, he was alive for Rob's Last Day.
Thank God.
Those Caesar stains on the ceiling always made me think of Rob.
"Thank you for employing me."

The Weatherman

It's Sunday.
We'll be open 285 Sundays, and I'll work 270 of them. I hate Sundays.
Sunday is a non-profit day. It will take 4 years worth just to get to break-even and pay myself the minimum wage!
And the clientele is different: Less English and more trouble! Each customer buys more but we're just not open enough hours to make it worthwhile. Sundays and holidays are the graveyard for people in retail.
Oh well, what can you do?

For some reason, I'm never quite ready for business at opening time, and I use the first hour to finish the prep work. The customer count is usually zero for this hour.
Sometime after 12 David Crosby walks up.

Not the real David Crosby of course, but his long lost cousin. Who probably can't sing and lives in a trailer park.

And who is the princess before me, with her rotting teeth and beer belly?

His wife.
Charming people.
"What can I do for you?"
"Extra Large Diet Coke. No ice!"
Emphasis on "No Ice."
I'm already sick of this guy. Relax. And your wife is glaring at me like she's demented.
I pick up the cup and walk over to the fountain machine.
Oops!
I knew I'd forgotten to do something this morning! Fill the ice chest.

The good old ice chest has to filled so the syrup lines are cooled to the point where even straight pop is cooled to a consumable temperature.
And it's pretty much empty.
Thirty-two ounces of this stuff and you'll be sick! The lines are insulated under the floor and it's at least the temperature of this stifling room.

I do my best Goody Two Shoes explanation of these facts to David and Godzilla, and suggest I put a few cubes in to make it taste OK.

Immediate and overwhelming resistance!

I only suggested the ice to them to bother them. God, they'd said "No Ice" so many times I thought they were a couple of white rappers.
I actually don't care that much, except these two are such vultures that I can't help toy with them a little bit.
They watch me dispense the drink with the intensity of boxing fans.
The cup now weighs a ton and collapses slightly. Some of the pop spills out on my hand and the counter.
I now get the "Fill It Up" glare from the guy.
I put more in, and this time I put it on the counter with two hands before I put the lid on.
Great. It's finally over. I'm $1.89 richer. Wow.

They leave.
Grouching about their pop.

THE MALL RAT

They buy food elsewhere and sit about 100 feet away.

They eat like bears, hovering over their kill. I can almost make out what's in the woman's mouth. And she keeps glaring at me. What a kook.

I disappear into the back room and try to forget about these cheapskates. I hate to have bad customers this early in the day because it sets a bad tone. Sometimes you get on a run of these types, sometimes 6 or 7 in a row that really push it. At "Lucky 7" I go out for a cigarette and wait until these customers have left our counter, eaten, and left the food court. 15 minutes. Then I take over and hopefully deal with a better crop.

Back out to the counter.

Oh no.

It's David Crosby again.

"This pop is warm—I want ice," he deadpans.

He's a tremendous actor. He's completely forgotten the "No Ice" song and dance routine he and Godzilla just performed.

Am I on one of those "Just For Laughs" segments?

He takes the lid off and pokes the cup in my face.

Gee, 60% of the pop is gone. Surprise surprise.

"You didn't want ice and you already have 2 drinks for the price of one. That's it."

"Ice!"

So now I have to give him as little ice as possible.

I make eye contact with him as I slip 3 ice cubes into the pop. The heat will melt them in 2 seconds anyway.

He's not fooled.

"More."

I try to do my best bewildered look, I have no idea what he means.

"More."

OK.

Just to piss him off I throw in 2 more cubes and put the lid on quickly.

"Here."

He's actually far angrier than he should be, and stomps off yelling to old Godzilla at the table.

They eventually leave. I've had my excitement for the day. May the rest of the day be bland and boring!

They got a free pop out of it. Oh well. They win. If you press hard enough, and don't mind looking ridiculous, you'll get something. They looked very poor, so I can rationalize this as an act of charity. Like Mother Theresa. Good Riddance. I mean God Bless.

Never to be heard from again.

Until the next day.

It's the Marketing Lady from the mall on the phone.

"I have a complaint about you."

Oh God no.

The Marketing Lady and I hardly ever cross paths.

But when we do, it's misery. She has a visceral, reflex hate for me! It's obvious and nasty.

The bottom line is that David Crosby is now apparently the weatherman on some TV channel and we are going to get some bad publicity!

This is silly.

He's not the weatherman on WKRP or whatever.

I'm trying to picture what kind of TV channel would have this guy as their weatherman.

And I can't.

I tell the Marketing Lady she's being conned.

She doesn't care because she now smells blood, a chance to make me look bad. So she informs me that I'm having a meeting with her and the General Manager of the Mall the next afternoon.

Great.

At this point I'm not too worried. There's obviously a big mistake here. I can see the con. This guy is good. But it'll get straightened out.

Fat Chance.

The next afternoon's meeting is Star Chamber justice.

The Marketing Lady is 100% convinced of Crosby's story. The General Manager is convinced the "weatherman" is going to slag the mall off on TV. Crosby had alluded to this.

THE MALL RAT

Sure, Sure.

"Tomorrow, it'll be 78 in L.A., 82 in Las Vegas, and by the way, don't go to Billy's in the mall. Those corrupt bastards wouldn't give me ice."

And these two are serious!

They tell me the mall has big advertising contracts with WKRP, and these are in jeopardy.

(Get out your violins.)

This is ridiculous.

I don't know how many times I try to make the same point.

He's not on WKRP.

He's not the weatherman.

Wake up, you deluded morons!

Compare my description with what he really looks like

Have him come to the mall to 'straighten it out." He won't appear.

Go to his mansion to straighten it out. It won't exist.

Never mind, I'm guilty. Down goes the hammer!

The Marketing Lady is loving this. I'm to write a Letter of Apology, and the mall will throw in some gift certificates.

That's the end of it.

No appeal to reason. No recourse. No nothing. I'm picturing this guy, back in his trailer home, opening up all kinds of freebies sent to him by people who've bought this "weatherman" story.

He probably is doing this, but takes time out of his busy schedule to phone Billy's Head Office with the same story and veiled threat.

Same result. More free stuff. More bad feeling.

So I lose.

On a $1.89 Diet Coke.

The "weatherman" gets enough to buy 100 Diet Cokes!

George Harrison said it best. "That's the way it goes."

That cup and 32 ounces of carbonated syrup will cause me infinite trouble.! Remember this one.

More than I Needed to Know

Sometimes you really know more then you need to.
Of all the information in this universe, some of it is better left unattended to. It will never cross your mind. It shouldn't.

It's whatever day of the week, shortly before lunch rush.
You never know what the crowd will be like on any given day. There are trends to even this aspect of fast food.
Well, that's not a good sign.
It's "Mr. Poofy."
I hate this guy.
He's really creepy.
He's about 60, 65, large cranium, little goatee, and earrings.
He always acts really poofy and gives me the creeps.
His wife is "Dame Creepy," so they make quite a pair.
I figure they met at a sex change clinic, and figured it wasn't worth the pain and expense to change into each other, so they left, happily ever after.
Who knows?
I picture him in a pink tutu on a flatbed in a Gay Pride Parade.
He's the one the crowd really gets into. Snapping his fingers. Groovy 60's dance moves.

He wanders over.

"I have diarrhea. I just crapped in my pants. They wouldn't serve me at the Taco place. Do you have a private bathroom where I can change into these clothes?," he asks, holding up a dept. store bag.

This is undignified. I should have stayed in school longer!

I'm about to serve food for 2 hours and this is more than I need to know right now.

"Heh. Heh. Wish I did. (not really.) No, there are no private bathrooms. The public ones are there. I believe there's a Men's and a Family one."

He's already aware of the public bathroom situation. He really believes I have a private bathroom.

"Does the Family one have private stalls?"

I just sort of mini-shrug and motion him off to the side. How would I know?

Fact is I don't really care. There are no bathrooms back here, and you should really just get Dame Creepy to drive you home. You're either too young or too old for this, so kindly remove yourself, and your soiled undies, from the premises.

He just gives me this pissed look, and saunters off to the bathrooms.

Yeesh.

Now, my mind goes where it shouldn't.

Men's or Family?

No, not the Family.

I've never been in there.

Actually, I went in there the last night of our occupancy! I figured a drunk Lyle had snapped off enough light fixtures in the food court, and then we entered the Family washrooms. Beautiful. Nice plush chairs. I couldn't bring myself to do anything bad, so I encouraged Lyle to piss all over them!

So I picture these horrified mothers recoiling in terror as this weirdo stalks in, incidentally smelling worse all the time.

He gives Mrs. Horrified an evil look and snatches the diaper out of her hand.

Then he raids the free amenities and disappears into a stall.

This would be pretty hard to take, as the room would soon be wafting of Poofy's mess.

This is not right.

It must have been a Mother's Determination that the occupants cleared the room before passing out!

No, he didn't go in there. I hope.

This guy left through the back exit doors. I didn't see the net result of his wardrobe change.

I can't imagine ever letting this guy use this fictitious bathroom.

"Hi, I have 2 fatal diseases. Can I stay at your house? Don't' worry, they're all contagious."

No, I can't.

And I really didn't appreciate his candor either.

But is was pretty funny.

I couldn't retell it without the recipient bursting into laughter. The problem with this is that the punch line comes at the beginning. As soon as you get to the "I have diarrhea" part, your audience loses it!

So, that's the story of Poofy the Pooh.

He did come back a couple of times.

I'd hide in the back, holding my ribs and wiping tears from my eyes.

No shame. "It's my right to crap in my pants!"

Way more than I needed to know.

And I'll leave you with a bad joke.

A: What kind of underwear do old people wear?

B: I don't know.

A: Depends.

Ha, ha (phony drum roll.) Brrum-Chah.

"Thank you folks. I'll be here in the Sunset Room all week. You've been a beautiful audience. Thank you. Thank you. Good Night."

Mr. D.I.Y.

When I took over this business, I really inherited a lot of junk.

The parsimonious owners bought everything second-hand or found it somewhere.

There was no sparkle and shine to anything. All the machinery made funny, unencouraging sounds that in translation meant upcoming expenses.

I used to joke with the staff that their ancestors must have toted some of this stuff across the prairies in chuckwagons.

I'd never seen so much duct tape in my whole life! Holding everything together. The "operational instructions" for some things would blow your mind. "Poke here, kick here."

At least the main signage and menu board were replaced when I took over.

Before that, it looked like some country bumpkins had set up viddle-shop in a city mall.

With the new sign I could at least walk by, and I didn't have to pretend like I didn't own the place.

Now at least the customers felt like they were eating at a legitimate establishment.

This sign was at least passable. It would be replaced again. Well into the

21st century Billy's had yet to discover the illuminated sign! So by the time we were leaving we finally had a proper sign. Yes, the world is a little maddening!

And of course I'm the least mechanically—minded person I know.
All these future repair jobs only gave me a heightened sense of anxiety.
To me, visegrips are my hands.
A hammer is anything handy.
I love glue for some reason, and always buy 3 different kinds to make sure the "project" is a success. The 3 kinds of glue usually end up mixed together. Then the inevitable 2- 3 day wait to see if the mess I've created hardens and holds together. It usually does.
If all else fails, hit the thing!
In school, we had to take industrial arts class. At family gatherings, my candle holder and piggy bank still draw uncontrollable laughter. Real conversation pieces.
For the most part, things held together. We were remarkably lucky. Although machines would make new, disconcerting sounds, they kept on going.

Malls are, in fact, dirty places.
Even if they look clean, they're dirty.
The amount of dirt in the air in these enclosed spaces would surprise you.
This dirt settles on your machinery.
Surprisingly fast.
So while I'm absolutely clueless when it comes to repairing anything, I try and go for preventative maintenance.
Any given fast food place has 10—15 pieces of equipment.
Equipment needs placing so you can access all parts of it. To clean it.
And air flow.
Cleaning plus air flow equals low repair bills. Simple equation.
But spaces in food courts aren't designed that way. The electrical outlets, gas mains, and so on, are placed in walls.
So placing your 10—15 machines in suitable places is near impossible!
That's why our cooler is under our front counter.
It's about 7' long, 2 ½ feet high, and 3 feet deep. Two doors. We supposedly keep milks and condiments in it. One of these units runs 3—4 K.

THE MALL RAT

That's a popular misconception people have about businesses. They think you get everything cheaper.

Actually, it's more expensive.

Food in restaurants is wholesaled at higher prices in many cases than what you pay in supermarkets. National contracts set prices, not the day to day market.

Prices of equipment don't reflect their relative value either. You've just gotta have the stuff to operate.

A plastic box called a grease trap costs $500-$700.

Instead of the $3K cooler, two $100 bar fridges would do the same job.

And this cooler stumps me.

No matter what I do, it won't work properly.

It's always warm.

I never really keep anything of importance in it.

It was actually the first piece of machinery to cause me a problem.

On the first Friday I owned the place, the thing got pushed or moved.

Which caused the hose running into the drain to bend. And back up. And flood. Everywhere. At lunchtime. What a circus!

And I'd only owned this dump for a few days, so I wasn't versed on all the do's and don'ts.

Like anything you survive, it's only funny afterwards.

But I won't give up on this cooler.

We come up with a plan to put some grills in the counter. It should be easy enough to take a piece out, and install a nice-looking chrome grill. It'll be down low anyway.

I let Stan take over the project.

He says it's a piece of cake.

Rather than put in a couple of ventilation holes, we'll just go for one big one, right down by where the motors run.

Sounds good to me.

Stan's a bit of a procrastinator, so I promise some beer on top of the cash payment for job completion.

Stan enlists his friend Tom to help.

Tom's a stoner. Every time I see him, he's wasted. I don't know how much help he's going to be, but his father apparently has a workshop with all the tools we'll need. Eventually, we'll crack off his drill bits and wreck his tools, but no matter.

    We're closed now. The lights are dimmed, the people gone. Time to set to work.
    Stan and Tom get down in front of the counter. And start to go at it.
    Hmm. Something's not right.
    I don't know what this counter is made of, but all I hear is drill bits breaking.
    Tom and Stan don't seem to get it.
    This isn't drilling through wood, this counter is made of some man-made substance that is meant to withstand heavy-duty public wear and tear.
    And they're making a real mess.
    Unhappiness is turning to panic. These stoned bozos better do something about this.
    I keep feeding them more beer. Out comes the sledge hammer.
    Stan starts beating on the counter. Tom and I are laughing at how hard Stan is beating on it. For absolutely no result.
    After we take turns beating on it for what seems an eternity, it is revealed that this counter is made of some kind of "plastic concrete" reinforced by some kind of rebar.
    It just won't surrender.
    It's like armor-plating.
    Who'd go to all this trouble to design counter material like this?
    Eventually, we tunnel through, beating, sawing and stabbing our way through.
    The hole is messy looking, but Stan screws the grill on. It's done.
    Doesn't look too bad!
    Too bad it doesn't work.
    Because it's a grill that has downward slots, no meaningful amount of air flow results.
    All that work for nothing.
    The "cooler" is still a "warmer."
    I'm sick of it.
    I don't want to pay the repair and maintenance bills any longer.

THE MALL RAT

The last straw is when I sink $600 into it to replace a motor, and it still doesn't get any colder.

The repair people guaranteed the work. I phoned them a couple of dozen times.

Then I gave up.

Get a new maintenance company.

And get rid of this cooler.

It's a pain in the ass.

I'll replace it with the aforementioned bar fridges. $100 each at Wal-Mart.

We are lucky in this city, there's a labor shortage, and the Health Dept. inspectors all seem to be former nurses from Eastern Europe. Their knowledge of restaurant regulations is thin at best, so they'll never even notice this violation.

But now I have to get rid of this clunker.

I'd like to wheel it right into the mall trash compactor.

It would probably break the compactor, which would land me in some kind of trouble.

So I abandon that idea.

The next idea is to throw it off the mall or a skywalk.

If you've never thrown an appliance off a building, you should. It's very gratifying. That crappy T.V. actually looks better in a million pieces. Higher the better.

But I'll probably get in some kind of trouble. My employees like the basic idea, but are afraid of the consequences.

I try to tempt them with making a drunken party out of it, but still they remain on the straight and narrow.

They don't know the fun of this kind of outing!

In college, a Frenchman, pretending to be a Bohemian, artsy type, was short of money.

He had a wine-colored early 70's Benz. A 2-series.

I know.

A 2-series.

What ugly tanks.

Everytime I see one, I look to see if I can spot a war criminal.

And now he's broke, so he wants to pay us $100 to "steal" it and trash it.

Hopefully never to be found.

"Stealing" it consists of him handing us the keys.

A good part of the $100 goes to the liquor store, and we divide the balance.

Off we go.

Up to the nearby back-country for a Dukes of Hazard episode.

I'll never forget the look of glee on my buddy's face as he rammed the car into a tree. Repeatedly. It was actually stuck. We unstuck it.

But at some point it dawns on us that this car is our only way back home.

So the demolition stops.

We drive it home with a piece or two hanging off. One or two of our manoeuvres really beat up the undercarriage.

"The car wouldn't die…so we couldn't abandon it…so here are your keys back. Bye."

Where's my $100?

That's a good question.

I believe "Gone" is the answer.

"Gone" as in you're never seeing it again, you crooked foreigner!

This really pissed him off.

In the end, at the end of the semester, on the day we were packing up to leave for the summer, he finally accepted a plaid shirt which was 3 sizes too big for him in lieu of "debt"!

See, this if all the fun we could be having. And you want no part of it!

So I guess I have to join the modern world and dispose of it at a designated dump.

And the way it goes today, I'll be jerked around and sent to some obscure location.

And I have to get it there.

I ain't got no truck.

So I'll have to rent one.

And pay.

And pay again at the dump.

And waste time.

And I'm a cheapskate.

And I only live about 20 minutes away by foot.

So I hatch this plan to wheel it to my house.

THE MALL RAT

Do it late at night.
Know the curbs and rises—I do anyway.
Should be easy.
Just add it to all the other junk in my shed and it'll eventually leave with the other stuff. Sometime.

So one night I stay after work. Preparing for the next day. About 10 o'clock I'm ready to roll.
It's kind of a suburban area so my route is pretty much abandoned at this hour.
A quarter of it will be parking lot anyway.
Only one intersection.
Easy.
Tape up the doors and hoses and we're all set.
Take a few beers from a unit that actually cools things, and I'm gone.
The parking lot is annoying.
Little rocks everywhere, and the wheels resist.
Stop. Chug. Move on.
Through an adjoining strip mall and gas station.
No one around.
There are a few cars around up ahead.
I just pretend I'm not doing this.
That way, this just isn't happening, and these kind folks will just mind their own business.
I could pretend to be a tree, but I don't want to push it, so I just freeze. No movement, no person. Sort of.
I wait until all cars are clear, and push it the rest of the way home. Uphill a little.
Maybe one car passes me.
I'm home.
Push it up the driveway.
Across the grass, but I'm 30 feet from my goal, and it's weightless.
Done.
Over.
A little more work than I thought, but it's done.

All that work has developed a powerful thirst!

I always over-buy at 2 places; the beer store and the candy counter.

So I still have a few cans left.

Many nights I wind down by going for a walk and chugging a few cold ones.

Don't worry, I'll never get caught.

Seriously, thousands of police cars have passed me by while I've been drinking a beer. I always do it. I'm lucky.

But not tonight.

I'm about a half mile from home when I see the police car.

Driving slowly.

Not particularly bothering with me.

I already know this part.

Put beer can in pocket. Make the bag of beer look like library books, and walk like a purpose-driven citizen.

They're not bothering with me at all. They've eyeballed me and have moved on.

Trouble is they won't leave the neighborhood.

I'm 10 minutes away from the house in one direction, and a field where I can hopefully lose them in the other.

So I keep moving.

I already know what's going on.

It's just taken them this amount of time to respond to the call from person who saw a guy pushing a cooler down the road!

Don't they know Mr. Do-It-Yourself?

I'm surprised the motorist didn't recognize me!

Now I have these 2 gumshoe hounds on my case.

Finally, Batman and Robin run out of leads and slow down near my position.

Down comes the window.

It's a woman cop.

It's Mr. and Mrs. Cop.

Good. People don't like to look bad in front of the opposite sex, so this is the best I can do.

Manipulation-wise, that is.

THE MALL RAT

"Good evening, sir."

"Hi, I bet you're looking for a man pushing a cooler…"

I go on to explain the whole thing to them, state that I don't want them to drive around wasting their valuable time, and wish them a pleasant evening.

They want to copy down my driver's licence information so I reach for it.

This is a little bit of a problem since I have a bag of beers in one hand, and an open one in the other in my coat pocket!

But I pull it off.

Never mind that I appear it be a left-handed person reaching into my front right pocket.

I always carry my wallet in my front right pocket. Travelling has told my to always carry your wallet in your front pocket. Eliminates money belts and pick pockets. Eliminates lots of things.

But apparently not stupid situations caused by nosy citizens with cellphones.

"What's in the bag?"

I first try to act like there's no bag.

Drowsy. Unresponsive.

"Ah, just stuff," says Mr. Cloudy.

"That's beer."

I'm trying to act stupid. Like I've never heard of beer.

I hold the bag sort of up to examine it.

Since I don't know what beer is, I give her a quizzical look.

She's not buying it.

"It's beer. Just like the beer in your other pocket."

She's looking at my pocket. Well, take out your hand.

Now I'm acting like I don't have a right arm.

She's not buying this.

But at least she thinks it's funny.

Mr. Cop isn't so amused. But I think he sees writing a long report for nothing.

I take my hand out of my pocket.

I don't have much to lose, and a ticket to gain.

I look at the beer like it's a U.F.O.

Mrs. Cop thinks I'm very funny.
So I avoid the ticket.
I'm told to finish the open beer immediately, and drink the rest at home.
I put the can to my head, and they leave.
Then I take it down and resume my walk and nice cold beers.

Most of the trying-to-fix-something stories ended in punctures, burns, clogged drains or worse.
At least this one ended successfully.
Nothing like a few cold beers after the completion of a well-thought out project.
Just remember to bring duct tape. And glue.
And the best way out of a ticket is to portray a calm "Oh well you got me" stance. One slight remorseful breath. Act dignified. A hint of contrition! You have a 50/50 chance. Advice from Mr. Do-It-Yourself.

The Coffee Fag

We served the worst coffee in the world.
No question about it.
Some cheesy brand. Bitter. Not nice.
The kind of coffee sold where you'd least expect it to be!
I used to get a laugh when new reps from the coffee company would come around!
They'd give us hundreds of dollars of free stuff, not realizing our account was worthless!
We started selling 3 cups of coffee a day, and finished at 7. In 5 years!

So who would drink this every day?
The Coffee Fag.

"Mr. Permanent Fixture."
First customer of the day.
For so long. Too long. Way too long.
This guy was a real trip.
Early 40's, scrawny, moustache, earring, and he walked with a limp.
The limp was from an industrial accident of some kind.

He was creepy, in a Manson kind of way.
But he was essentially harmless. I hoped.

And part of his daily routine was to come to the mall, limping along, and buy coffee from me.
Why?
He had a crush on me!
I cringe at the thought!
And I had to serve him day after day after day.

At some point in the sale he'd give me a really piercing look.
It was just part of his day.

Get up, go to the mall for the best coffee in the world!

I saw him once in the parking lot, getting out of a rusted mid 70's Blazer.
The other time I saw him he was picking cigarettes butts up off the sidewalk!
He didn't seem the cigarette picker-upper type, but hey, there's a lot you don't know about Mr. Interesting here. And he said the same lines every day.
I tried not to ever picture him, but Lyle could imitate him perfectly. It was quite funny, I must say.

By now you can figure out that Billy's is a bit of a Sunset Grill.
Henley hit the mark there.
And the Coffee Fag is one of the characters. Henley is so observant. I wonder if he ever logged a shift or two inside. He would have had fun.

It's whatever day of the week.
I'm in one of my ill-advised experiments!
This one entails giving the staff more responsibility!
My exercise in futility "du jour" is letting Len open the store for me in the morning.
This isn't a video game, so Len isn't making much progress. And the first customer of the day arrives. Guess who?

THE MALL RAT

But Len doesn't know what he's doing, and the till hasn't been put into the cash register yet.

So Lazy Len decides to have a moment of Customer Appreciation and gives the Fag a free one!

"Bout time I got something free. This is the worst coffee I've ever had!"

He actually said that.

After 500 cups!

Like I said, he'd come with his 95 hard-earned cents and look at me.

Sometimes he came twice a day. No matter. It was out of the same batch as the first one anyway!

The ordering conversation was always the same, so I gradually could serve him without making much eye contact.

Once in awhile he'd look at me in an even stranger way. And then blush. Or mumble.

I used to have a running gag with any new employees who'd buy it.

As the Coffee Fag was always around, I used to try and convince any new employee that it was him "C.F." was coming to see.

Some of them bought it. The look of horror on their faces was a guaranteed knee-slapper.

Or they'd act paranoid around him. That was good, too.

And this was the guy's routine for a long, long time.

"This is the worst coffee I've ever had."

Worst Coffee: 95^{cents}
Best Line of all Time: Priceless
Down at the Sunset Grill.

50 Ways to Ask for Water

Water.
H2O.
No profit. Unless bottled. Heavy. "Messy."
Pop is profitable. Pop is good. Pop defines . . .
But just when the world is running out of something, everyone loves it. Like water.
Don't get me wrong, water is a great drink.
At home.
In the high-rent world of malls, passing out water is not a good thing.
Unfortunately, our previous owner attracted an el cheapo clientele. That was the atmosphere of the place.

And water was the drink.
I hated water.
Besides not being a money maker, you had to pay for the cup plus clean up the mess.
And people who ask for water never look you in the eye. Real rats.
We sometimes used to pretend we'd never heard of "water."
We'd make them describe this "water," and then we'd still feign ignorance of this substance.

THE MALL RAT

Act like a Lawyer.

I pushed one lady too far and she stood there and screamed "WATER" at me. With about five people looking at me, I finally "UNDERSTOOD."

"Oh yes, of course. A glass of water."

For every argument in favor of water, I had a counter-argument.

"It hydrates you."

"Actually, it only makes you thirstier."

And I purposely ordered these ridiculously small cups.

My favorite was to try and convince people water and fried food don't mix.

I'd look at them with the authority of a doctor. At least a T.V. doctor. And then give them some scientific mumbo-jumbo about how soft drinks interact with greasy enzymes, (whatever they are), in a positive way. Positive as in negative.

The Doubting Thomases still wanted their Adam's Ale.

So, I leave you with "50 Ways to Ask For Water." Don't use any of them. Thank you.

Just Water.

A glass of the "City's Best."

I'll have my usual . . . 5 large glasses of water! (Never seen him before.)

Where's the water?

Adam's Ale, sonny.

For my drink I'll have . . . ah . . . oh . . . ee . . . just a glass of water.

Does it come with water?

I hate pop, give me water.

Water. Where's my water? You "forgot" the water.

I work in a bottling plant. Gimme me tap water.

H20.

I need to take a "pill."

Can I have an empty cup?

Refill?

I forgot to order drinks!!! Just water. No need to go to any extra "trouble."

What's that "stuff"? Can I have some?

Same as her.
Those fruit juices cause cancer, gimme water.
You make good money on pop, gimme water.
My "Dad" needs some water.
My distant relative 10 times removed needs water.
Where's the fountain?
By law you have to give us water with our food.
The place next door won't give me a free refill! Can I have a glass of water?
Can I bother you for a glass of water?
We're water people.
Just fill "it" with water from that thar "machine."
Can you fill my water bottle?
I need to clean that table. Can I have a cup of water?
Customer grabs pop cup and gapes around.
I'll buy a pop, unless you have water.
Where did that man get that cup of water?
(Holding throat), I need water!!
I'm thirsty, do you have water?
Plastic bottles in our landfills, gimme a cup of water.
Tryin' to sell me something, I'll stick with water.
You didn't ask if I wanted water.
Oh, and Buttercup, why don't you ask the nice man for some water.
(Gets cup of water). Gulp. More.
Do you give out free water like the "other places"?
Water's good enough for me!
Me too!
(Chewing like a horse) Mmm, what's missing?
And this young man's going to give us some water.
It's hot in my store, can I have some water?
Nothing to drink, only water.
Got a tap back there?
Oh look, just enough (?), I'll have to have water.
Do you think I could have something to wet my whistle?

WATER!!!!!
Don't worry. I know you'd count!

The Best Night Ever

There are good bosses, and bad bosses.
Mostly bad.
I've dealt with some very comical and arbitrary people in my time. One boss thought he was the reincarnation of Confucius!
I don't know about that, but I know I've been in the presence of the reincarnation of Mr. McGoo several times.
That's why I'm self employed.
And one of the perks of being the boss is command over the entertainment budget.
You can honestly claim a certain amount for entertainment, and because I have no business associates to actually entertain, I simply blow the money on my employees.

So every quarter, on a Saturday night, we'll shove off from Billy's and go on a bender.
Multi-venue nights with a good variety of "experiences" are the best ones.
And we usually include a few alumni. They all know each other anyway.
My enduring image of these nights is when I get out of the cab and look

back. When I look back, I usually see an inebriated Reg pressed to the cab window, wanting the fun to go on forever!

One night our cabbie took a left turn and proceeded down the wrong side of the road. With a cement lane divider!

Everyone was drunk, but I realized it right away.

I let him drive along until I saw the oncoming car lights.

Then I calmly asked if he realized he was on the wrong side of the road!

He ditched into an apartment building driveway and turned around.

Lately, in the newspaper, there have been a few articles about the impending closure of a well-known dive in the downtown core.

This hotel has been around for 80 or 90 years, but it's now the worst area of town.

The cops go there 10 times a day.

Murders, homeless everywhere, drugs, you name it.

Sounds like the perfect night out, if I do say so myself.

A sociological experiment, a living history night.

So I mention this to Lyle, who agrees that this is a "worthy" endeavour.

We set the night, and recruit our posse.

There'll be 5 of us—me, Lyle, Len, Reg and Scottie Evil. Scott's a Goth with a girlfriend named Egypt. Need I say more.

Lyle and I have to work until 8 on Saturdays, so we tell the others to meet us at 9 at a nearby pizza chain.

We'll cab it from there.

I try to play a little psychology and tell them not to turn up until 9.

I'm not cheap, but this isn't what we're really doing tonight, so no use in getting too comfortable there. Or ringing up a huge bill.

Lyle and I get into the beer about 7.

On nights like this, you can always count on the 7:59 customers. Always.

So we finally cut out. Its 8:10. Quick Change Quentin and we're at the pizza place.

One of them burps, "Been here for hours."

The empty pitchers and plates confirm that my staff didn't buy into my psychology.

I didn't expect them to!

THE MALL RAT

Lyle and I are already a case of beer into it, so we order enough to cover everyone and pour it all down.

But now we've wasted a little bit too much time here, so I'm on everyone to leave.

I get the bill, shake my head, laugh, and then rally them out the door.

Cab time.

I hate technology, and those teenagers with cell phones and other devices fail to get us a cab.

I have no faith in any of this stuff anyway. It's all fakery on T.V. commercials. In real life, you'd be stuck in the middle of nowhere crunching this thing under your heel.

And there's nothing worse than being drunk with the next beer nowhere in sight!

So I resort to my old school methods and hop out to the main road to flag a cab down.

It's a huge road, and I manage to cross the 6 lanes without getting killed.

The old international hand signal will surely get us a cab.

And it does.

The cabbie thinks I'm the only passenger.

You wish.

I bellow at the 4 hand-held device carrying youths and they make their way across the road, and pile into the cab.

"Oh no, no. Too many."

"Who's counting? We won't tell anyone."

"No, No. It's against the law. My fellow drivers will report me if they see this."

"That's not going to happen. You're going to drive us to this hotel and I'm going to pay you twice the meter."

Greed takes over, but he still doesn't want to do it.

I'm a firm believer in ignoring rules that don't really work for me.

I'll stop at a light at 4:30 a.m., but if there's no one around, I'll proceed.

If I have an open can of beer, I'll take it from one place to another. As long as I'm not the driver.

Then I'll have a passenger hold it until we arrive at the next destination.

Mr. Bad Example.

Well, there's only one way to get this guy to drive us.
And that's to trick him.
"If I can guess what country you come from, will you drive us?"
"Yes."
"Ethiopia"
"How did you know?"
I don't really know how I know, but I can't let on that I'm not exactly a psychic.
"I win. Drive."
One of the boys ducks down to satisfy the situation, and we're off.

The tip factor looks good, until we near our destination.
Now our cabbie is getting nervous.
"I go no further."
"It's still 3 or 4 blocks."
He stops the car. "No further."
I do see his point.
It's a bit of a combat zone.
A second or two ago someone walked by with a clown's nose on!
Oh well, we're close enough.
This is one of the most entertaining walks ever!
It's so run down.
Junkies, homeless, the living dead.
Lyle stops to relieve himself, only to be informed that he's urinating on someone's "house."
I compensate the aggrieved flood victim, and we're off.

Len and Lyle are nervous the whole evening—S. Evil, Reg and I love it. We're right in our element.
Reg lived on the streets once, so he had some interesting commentary about it all.
Dumpster Diving, staking your turf, it all sounds so primal.

And there she is, the Grand Old Lady.
About to meet the wrecking ball.
There's at least 100 people in front of this dump.

THE MALL RAT

They're the ones too down and out to even get in this fleahole.
It's Crack City.
What a collection we have here.
Actually, we should be afraid.
But we aren't. There are 5 of us, enough to subdue any disoriented crackhead. We hope.
And I don't think the crowd really likes us much.
To them, we're a scummy lot of middle-class whites down to make fun of them. We're college kids on a lark.
We stop and make a few new friends. Pass out a few smokes and the odd greenback and you're safe.
I can see why you'd want to demolish this whole area.
But I like drinking in all kinds of places. Dance halls are too predictable. I like Hell's Angels and talking to old geysers who won't even remember you when they sober up. "She was my old lady…"

We finally make our way to the doors.
There's no reception area. What an innovative hotel idea.
A dingy downward staircase takes you to somewhere.
The stairs are littered with more bums, and the bathrooms are packed with diseased, urinating creeps.
I must say it is rather horrible. Perhaps we have bitten off more than we can chew. Len and Lyle really aren't into this.

We finally run the gauntlet and are now in the bar and entertainment "room."
It's quite large, the whole basement of this place.
The only problem here is that there are less than 10 customers in this huge space.
You have to buy something, so there are no people here. I can see why this place is going under.
Oh well, at least the service will be better!
Not likely.
The "waiter" won't serve us unless I bribe him.
He tries to tell us he has no product, or something.
Whatever.

This person is a drug addict, or drug addict in recovery, so I don't want to push our luck too far. He's really abrasive and even gives us the "Shove the beer up your ass" attitude when he finally delivers. This takes forever anyway.

Food?
I saunter over to the kitchen area, where Mrs. Heroin is standing, wondering where she is.
I try to engage her in a meaningful conversation about the availability of food.
I soon give up.
It's like I'm talking to an alien.
This place sucks and I'm glad it's closing!

One of the ten patrons is a single man alone over by the wall. He's sitting facing it.
Twice he comes over to us and asks us when the "entertainment" is going to "start."
There's not a band in this world desperate enough to come here.
And play to who?
It's the place itself that's interesting. Eating and drinking here is a bust. Not that we need to—we're all "3 sheets to the wind anyway." We need 5 brains to do the work of one.

The "Laws of Cab Availability" says we ain't riding out of here.
So we hoof it out of the hotel, and get to the subway station.
Next stop: Strip Club.
After the thrills for the homeless, we might as well do something "fun."
We pour ourselves on to the train and ride out of the ghetto.

I'm not big on strip clubs.
The whole idea of it baffles me.
"Perv Row" especially brings me down.
There's Phil the Postman putting bills in the G-string of "Cherries Galore," or whoever.
He's dreaming of she being his little wifey. Back at his basement apartment.

THE MALL RAT

In a week or two Miss Galore will disappear. She'll be in the next town. She's now "Sunny Bunny" or "Katja Lookin" or something. And there's Phil the Maintenance Guy from the airport. In Perv Row. Dreaming.

Oh well, I shouldn't be so skeptical.

They're selling, you're buyin'.

And the boys enjoy it.

Reg loves it, so does Stan when he's with us.

Reg likes a good cigar and a prime seat in Perv Row.

Lyle and I usually play pool and try to disassociate ourselves from the scene. Especially when the boys buy those ridiculous autographed pictures. "Forever in my dreams, xxoo, Dark Lady."

It's absolutely inane, but I guess I can just grin and bear it.

It's early morning now. Time to say goodbye to Misty and Thyme and hit the road.

After we try to communicate our various destinations to the cabbie, it's homeward bound.

Reg's face is pressed to the window of the cab.

It's been a long haul since early evening at Billy's.

I'm about $500 lighter.

For staff outings, we had a lot of fun.

This one was the Best Night Ever.

A Day in the Life of Devin

Life's like a box of chocolates.
If only.
It's more like a box of dried prunes.
Which one is going to taste "less-shitty"?

And so it goes with employees.
They show up looking for a job.
You do a little tap dance, see if you need what this person is pretending to be, and then it's "yay" or "nay."
I could write a book on the Art of Approaching a Sceptical Boss, but I won't.
But please bring a pen to the "interview"!
And in response to questions regarding how you would benefit the place, don't write "Because I'm Super-Duper."
More like a "Super-Doper" by the look of you. Do you have eyes?
Wash. Don't bring your friends. Or your mommy.
I hate the Mommy Episodes.
I've had a few.

THE MALL RAT

This Mother-Son duo used to come to the food court.
The son was about 16 and looked really gay.
There are good gays, and bad gays.
This is a bad gay. He's fickle and weird.
They came to our place because sonny-poo likes our mushy peas. Not fish. Not fries. These horrible peas.
Need I go on.
And one day they enquire about a job for the son.
Our "Help Wanted" sign is always up.
We give them an application.
I have no intention of giving this gay, I mean guy, a job.
No way.
He's a creepy fairy from the Land of Wearing Mommy's Clothes.
Not a chance.
But they come around to buy some peas and check on the status of this imaginary job.
The mother is very well dressed and my guess, from the beady, penetrating eyes, that she's a lawyer. A nasty one.
So I just keep fobbing them off.

Until I'm not there one night, and good old Stan has to deal with them.
Mr. Diplomat tells them we can hire whoever we want!
That has a lot of different meanings, especially if you're talking to a lawyer.
So she threatens Stan with some kind of civil rights lawsuit!
You idiot.
At least she backs off and never comes back.
They still come to the food court, but not to our place.
The kid eventually gets a Sunday job at a restaurant attached to the mall.
As a garbage hauler.
I'm glad I didn't hire him.
All he has to do is push a garbage trolley on wheels. He looks like he's going to die!
If you die, please be assured Mommy Dearest will get the maximum award.
This is the worst case scenario, but when Moms show up it's a bad way to start.

And so I hired Devin.

He showed up with Mom one day.

Her look of desperation said, "Please, please take him off my hands."

Devin looked like a younger version of the guy in "Ernest Goes to Camp."

A semi slack-jawed yokel type.

And he'd never, ever make eye-contact with you unless he was speaking to you.

And since he only ever said "Yup," your contact with him and his world was sort of, yes, that's it. Minimal.

This was a strange job interview.

She was doing all the talking, and he was like a puppet that came to life every once in a while with a "Yup" and a look.

Devin's story was that they came from a town up north, and that he'd previously worked at another outlet of our chain.

I think they sensed I thought he was a bit of a vegetable, so Mom told me about a not-too-specific industrial accident Devin had purportedly been in.

He looked fine to me, so I figured this was part of the story to cover up a rehab story.

Luckily, his parents had rescued him while he could still say "Yup"!

So Devin was my new cook.

Because he already knew the menu, which I doubted, he really had no reason to talk to me.

Every attempt at conversation or instruction was met with yet another "Yup."

Lyle hated him.

And he hated Lyle.

Lyle wanted to hit him.

I cautioned Lyle against this.

In this state, there's a 3-month probation period, so I can ditch Devin in the next 90 days. No questions asked.

A person who says nothing and never looks at you tends to creep you out.

I want to ditch him soon, but as I look at the calendar I see an obvious problem.

THE MALL RAT

My brother-in-law wants to go to the Super Bowl.
The 90 days runs just about at this time, so let's get through Christmas, and then see about tickets.

In the meantime, back at the farm, Devin still hasn't said anything.
He's a strange guy.
He's too stupid to cook when you verbally call the order.
He waits until the ticket is on the chit-board, and then extends like a cobra to within 4 inches of the ticket and squints to see what's on it!
Over and over.

And he's eating me out of house and home.
My policy is to let the employees eat whatever during the shift. Use common sense.
Devin has no common sense.
I sense that part of the rift between Devin and his family is that he doesn't eat with them.
He eats at work.
A lot.
And he's fixated on our good but expensive chicken fingers.
They are the most expensive item in terms of food cost.
And he's eating them wholesale!
Two meals each shift, plus these covert snacks which result from "accidentally" cooking too much product. Oops, I'll just have to eat-it.
Not to mention you shouldn't be snacking while cooking.
I don't know which pisses me off more—watching him do this or watching him eat in the back.
In the back, he stares vacantly while he chews like a camel!
And he always stares at a box of Coke cups up on the shelf.
What he's divining from the Coke cups I have no idea.

He's a total idiot.
I'm going to go bankrupt if this guy keeps eating all this chicken!
Maybe he'll sprout wings and fly away!
No luck.
He keeps eating chicken fingers.

I finally tell him no more chicken fingers. Anything else, OK.

My food policy hinges on the fact that the employee will eventually get tired of the food, and slowly eat a normal amount, or, in many cases, nothing at all.

So, what does he do?

If you guessed that he now takes fish and cuts them and moulds them to resemble chicken fingers, fries them and eats them, then you'd be right!

And he's still staring vacantly at the Coke cups.

He's a total lunch pail.
And a slow cook.
And my brother-in-law is closing in on the tickets.
Devin shows no sign of life.

But I do make him do something repulsive once.
Kill a mouse!
To our credit, mice are at a minimum at Billy's.
It's a miracle.

We are quite near the trash compactor, and our immediate neighbour is one of the dirtiest tenants in the food court.

As an operator, you take your pick.

It's either spend money on maintenance, or on repairs.

The neighbor's a repair guy! Deluxe Version.

No maintenance ever.

So the place is filthy.

One morning, I'm in the smoking area and one of their employees comes out of the back doors.

With a mouse! By the tail!

This so-called employee tells me it's been in the sink all night, but they don't have the whatever to kill it, so they're letting it go. Out here.

Brilliant.

So we've been pretty lucky.

But today there is a mouse.
It's up front.
And it's lunch time.

And I'm here with Devin.
And this mouse is really distracting.
And it's only a matter of time before a customer sees it.
The stupid mouse finally gets between 2 french fry boxes pushed along the wall.
If I get land another box on the outside, the mouse is trapped.
I do.
Mission accomplished.
At least the mouse is contained.
This is for a long time.
Over an hour.
We have to wait until all customers are gone before we can do anything about it.
I come over and check on the mouse periodically.
It's still alive and kicking.
It won't be for long!
A checklist of what we have on hand yields the fact that we have nothing suitable for this job.
So I've decided that Devin is going to bludgeon the mouse with an expendable old broom in the closet.
And then clean up the mess.
It's only right.
I'm the boss.
I'll be firing this mutant soon anyway.
After the crowd dies down, I inform him of his "promotion" in the organization.
He's not overly impressed, but he's too stunned to say "no" either.
"Yup."
And away he goes.
I forgot that his eyesight isn't very good, so he ends up making a mess out of the mouse.
Oh well, it's done. Now clean it up.
Finally, our beloved Super Bowl tickets come through.
A quick look at the calendar tells me I will have Devin on the schedule that runs until the day I leave.
A new schedule will have no Devin.

No more Lyle threatening to quit or kill him.
No more "fingers" of any kind.
No more "Yup."
No more staring at those stupid cups.
It'll be his 80-somethingth day. Just in time.
I'll just put up the new schedule on the afternoon of my last day, and axe him at close.
Simple.
It's not working out, blah, blah, blah. See you later.

The day comes.
I'm now thinking about the Super Bowl.
Firing Devin is like a detail.
Pack shirts. Check weather in Houston.
Fire Dufus.
So I put up the schedule.
Devin looks at it multiple times with this perplexed look on his face.
I've got to pull the trigger.
Lyle's expecting to turn up tomorrow morning with Devin gone!
It's now closing time.
I give him the little talk and fire him.
He's not getting it.
I point at the schedule.
"You no on it" sort of thing.
He's still not getting it.
Holy Jesus.
This is like the SNL skit where the director guy is telling the actor he's the worst actor he's ever seen. And he's not getting it.
Only that's funny, and this isn't.
Can someone kick Rasputin here through the ice?
Where's the guy with the cane when you need him?
I speak slower.
Still no comprehension.
This idiot's a real idiot.

In my mind, I'm now at the game. I hear Janet Jackson's going to perform.

THE MALL RAT

With Justin Timberlake.
(Actually the streaker was better. He wasn't shown on T.V. It was very funny when he started to run up the field and got clotheslined by one of the Panthers.)
Lynn Swann is going to sign my program at the airport.
I will be in Steeler Heaven.

But right now I have to fire this clown!
I'm starting to feel that I've done everything I can.
I really have to go.
If he shows up tomorrow, what can I do?
I go over it one more time.
I see some flicker of life in his eyes.
I take this as acknowledgement of all I've said.
I walk him to the door.
"Come by for your pay, bring back the company shirts. Blah, blah. Nice knowin' ya."
He's out the door now.
Hallelujah!
And then he turns to me.
"So, when's my next shift?"
"This was the last shift."
And I close the door.

I think his Mom called to "straighten it all out."
I wasn't around.
No sirree.
Yup.

The Drool King

Customers can provide free entertainment.
If someone different walks up, your brain may be engaged in an instant "wonder" moment. This possibility had never existed before! This had never occurred to me before!
One customer had an operation and had 3 nostrils for a while! I once sat next to a leper on a bus and he had no nose, only a gnarly hole in his face.

And one morning the Drool King came to visit me.
Customers who show up shortly after you open always rate high on the Interesting Scale. A lot of them are on the tail-end of a bender!
A nice little old man. Scraggy for sure. Wears one of those thick, plaid Lumberjack-type jackets. He's kind of smelly.

And what's that?
What is that?
I want to laugh, but in the best interests of this sale I'd better not.
This guy has a Brooklyn Bridge of spit connecting the corner of his mouth to the corner of the lapel on his jacket.
I hope it doesn't drop on my counter or Coke machine or anything!

But it has to drop sometime!
It wavers. It quivers. It dangles. It flexes.
But it doesn't drop.
If he talks, it moves.
If he moves his head, it goes right along with him.
This is impossible.
A magician couldn't do this.
This is the most interesting elastic saliva I've ever seen!

And he's oblivious to this bridge of drool!
Can't he feel it?
It must weigh something.
Nope.
And it starts to droop.
But then he moves his head and it snaps back to attention!
He could sell this as an act, but I don't think his saliva could be that cooperative.
I wonder what he ate to produce this? Perhaps a nice syrupy pop?
Whatever his secret is, this is the longest suspended saliva in the world.
No cartoonist would attempt this. Sooner or later it would have to drop.

One morning I walked in on Stan making coleslaw, and drool was dropping out of his mouth into the tub of slaw!
He had a vacant, brain-dead look at his face. No expression whatsoever. I burst out laughing. He wasn't trying to do anything malicious, he was just that zombie-like.
Luckily, I happened upon this, and threw the contaminated product out!
If you pay peanuts, you get monkeys. Who drool.

But this bridge would not fall.
It was like a spider's web in its simplicity and strength.
But the novelty was wearing off. Time to move along to the next stall at the circus kind-of-thing.

Thankfully, a young female now comes up to the counter to help this man.

It looks like his daughter or granddaughter.
She'll covertly take out a tissue or something and quietly save his dignity. We'll all be old someday ourselves.
But of course she doesn't notice a thing.
I'm really agog at this!
There is really no readily available explanation for this.
Maybe she's just pretending it's not there, so it's not there. It works.

Or maybe she's a hustler and she picked this old relic up at the bus stop and she's workin' him for some free grub. Who knows?

Anyway, it's time for them to go.
It's still hanging there.
We cook our food to order, so he's been standing there over 4 minutes.
You'd think the chemical composition of this thing would change and it would eventually collapse.
Or it would just slide down his beard and jacket.
No chance. No way.
He's thanking me and the bridge is moving up and down, mimicking his verbal thank you.
Get lost, please.
I've had it with this. I'm barely awake and I'm forced to watch this song and dance.
I note that his worthy assistant has whisked the food away to a table.
He's so slow that she's "disappeared" before he can even turn around. He spots her over yonder and tries to "run."

And that's the end of him. He and his saliva have departed.
I can finally laugh. Suppressing laughter is a must for the fast food business.
I hope she enjoyed the food.
He might have got a nibble!
Or sat there.
Drooling.

Stalkers

Sweet dreams are made of these
Who am I to disagree?

Travelled the world and the Seven Seas
Everybody's lookin' for something.

True, Annie. Everybody's lookin' for something.

Stalkers, female ones, I guess, are a product of the modern world.
The insular nature of society, technology and negative idea reinforcement, and the birth of the woman's movement are "plausibles" for this trend. People have very fertile minds.
A lot of people are genuinely creepy. (I once had a stalker ask me if I thought she was creepy).

You only need a couple of ingredients for Stalker Stew. Here's how you make a stalker.
First, you need a stick of Attraction.
Add a generous pinch of Fantasy.
And boil it all in a pot of Location.

Serve hot!

Hey, if someone knows you get out of your car at 10pm every night, guess where they're going to be? Fifty feet away.

If you have a location, and schedule, then you're in business.

I've been stalked, and interestingly enough, I've seen other people stalked. To see it in a sort of detached way, to watch someone else being stalked, gave me some insights into the subject. Particularly from the point of view of the futility of it all, based on the fact that I knew something of the life of the person being stalked, and knew this stalker had no future there.

You got Location. You got Attraction. It's the Fantasy part that's troubling.

And this involves the stalker believing that the world began when they showed up on the scene. The instant attraction, this is what they now want, they have some fantasy churning in their minds. It's YOU and THEM. It's "Love" to them.

And of course this can run the whole scale from innocent infatuation and interest to people who want to put you in a snuff movie! You don't know.

All you know, as the prey, so to speak, is that you pay rent here, do business here, and this person keeps turning up for another performance. And another.

They're remarkably the same, but of course also unique and the question is always what are they really doing, what are they really after?

In the above case, where I could watch someone else being stalked for a long period of time, I asked her if it worried her.

She replied that this person was very lonely, had virtually no friends, and was harmless.

True, except for the harmless part. You never know.

One of my employees also had the stalker mentality. Driven, totally blind to the fact that the intended recipient of your love hated and feared you. Calculating and observant personalities.

Put this cast of folks together and you really can't bet on much.

THE MALL RAT

When I took over the business, the thought of stalkers never crossed my mind. I was Joe-Business Guy, nothing more. The thought of women, and a few men, coming around in various routines never crossed my innocent little consciousness.

I suppose the reader needs a reason as to why these people would stalk me in the first place, what could possibly be that appealing?

Who knows? Maybe I own a "business," or maybe it's my eyes?

Over the 5 years there will be about 40 hardcore women. And a few unwanted men.

They range in age from 18-45. Some last a short time, some from "Day 1" to the end.

All colors.

To each of them, I represent some kind of fantasy.

Some are restrained and respectful.

Some are nasty.

You learn something every day.

Guess which day of the week stalkers like?

Friday. A show I saw once mentioned that serial killers also like Friday.

It's either the end of the week, or the start of the weekend. Time to check in!

My record there was 6 or 7, depending if you count the perma-stalker working across the way! On a Friday.

Lyle was the only person who knew all these women. We had nicknames for a lot of them. He'd tell me when they came around, sometimes they'd ask the wrong people information about me. And that was always funny.

And on that Friday, Lyle asked me how even I could keep them all straight! The looks, the plot. It's actually easy, the eyes do all the work.

On that Friday, 2 of these women almost walked into each other! That was weird. Literally missed each other by 2 feet and half a second! With the perma-stalker looking on!

All three blissfully ignorant of the others! When you look at one, only that connection exists. And that's when you see the unrealness of it all.

What one is doing, someone else is doing literally a couple of feet away.

Based on the fact that I'm not going to be involved in 3 "Happily Ever Afters" simultaneously, this scene is a little crazy. Just a little.

This was the heyday, about halfway through my ownership. One day, we counted up a list of 18. Current. Lyle enjoyed the sideshows.

Inevitably, some were never seen again. At the same time, you'd never know when some new woman was going to arrive. And maybe never leave! You never knew.

All you could say was that if any of this group was near or in the mall, you'd be having a visitor.

Another of my observations is about their level of seriousness. I'd say, based on things they showed me, the way they acted around others, and so on, that probably 5-7/40 of these women had something on the go. Sometimes this would be revealed after they had finally settled on some man, and the "joint appearance" would say a lot. It's all flattery.

Again, you can establish patterns about people. The M.O. is the same in a lot of cases.

Only you can't guess the motivation level and plans.

I only wish to comment on women who stand-out, for one reason or another.

Who was the first?

The "Original Butterface."

Butterface. Everything's good, "but-her-face." Actually she had a pretty face.

And the jeans and t-shirt body of a beer poster chick.

And she literally threw it all across the counter at me on, like, Day 5. She was forward. She leapt at me. Wasn't expecting that! Rob gave her a nickname, and it stuck to the end. Because she was there until the end.

She eventually would stop ordering our food, and everyone else's, for dietary reasons!

Instead, she'd park herself, usually by herself, and eat her bag lunch and stare at me for a good 40 minutes. That's an eternity, as the average person eats in 6.

Every 10-14 days. Forever.

She was in a trance. Fantasyland.

She had a cute little squint. As chance would have it, she worked for the optometrist. Or should I say "As Chaucer would have it"!

But at least she was harmless.

THE MALL RAT

I represented whatever it was I represented, something she presently didn't possess.

Lyle tried to break her gaze once, and concurred in the trance thing.

But she was harmless.

I must say I've never had anyone stare at me for such a prolonged period of time.

I crossed paths with her once in the parking lot. At a four-way stop. Her head literally coiled to the front windshield, like a snake to the snakecharmer!

Yes, the Original Butterface. Not to be confused with any other Butterfaces!

She eventually got braces to straighten out the one tooth my staff cited as the basis for her nickname.

Like I said, I thought she was hot anyway.

The creepiest was Stacey. I found that woman that worked in the mall, were, for obvious reasons, the worst ones to control and deal with. They have a "legitimate" reason to be in the mall, and have access to all areas. This girl was truly out there.

One has to remember that, while this person is stalking you, in some cases these women are clinical sex maniacs, and they're pursuing everyone.

And she was.

It's funny when a girl is really pouring it on, and you already know things about her and her life.

Things like venereal diseases.

Little things like that.

I would try to not even breathe the same air as her! I hated to be stuck with her having a smoke outside the back doors.

And you knew stuff about her that would make her stares even scarier because you knew what she was thinking!

Or you thought you did!

Having a smoke one day, she must have been in an exceptionably crazy mood and looked at me seriously and said, "I'll pay you the same as a high-priced hooker if you let me tie you up and beat you."

Not even whip. Beat!

It was easy to decline and remain composed. I hate pain. Needles, pills, even doctors. Stacey tried to convince me by telling me that she really wanted to do it, and it would be fun!

I wasn't reassured.

Chances are you'll end up as a chained-up freak in her "playroom."

Worse still, you'll be on the 6 o-clock news as they rescue you, dazed from your 2 years in captivity!

That smoking area proved to be a place where bad things happened.

The girl in question this time had an interesting quality. Her eyes would actually twinkle, like in the cartoons. Can't recall seeing that too many times. You couldn't do it if you tried.

This girl was in LOVE.

I'm trying to wake up, have my coffee, and a smoke.

It's 8:30.

She arrives.

Out of nowhere she tells me that she wants to marry me, and that she'll make me "so" happy! Her logic is that her long-time boyfriend wants to get married, but he's not good enough to have children with.

She's serious.

I'm flabbergasted!

In retrospect, I really have to give this chick high marks. It's deal-closing time at the OK Corral, but she's going to throw a "Hail Mary."

I try to be gracious and mumble something about being taken.

She eventually married the guy and they have a child or two.

Every time I saw her after that, there was a bit of a feeling of uneasiness.

She eventually disappeared.

I thought about her one day.

She appeared about 2 days later with a kid! I saw her with the child and husband a couple of times. He looked so happy. She not quite so.

Of the three mentioned so far, the only one I'd class as truly corrupted nympho material was Stacey. And girls like this love malls, it's their playroom, their grounds. And you see these girls actively patrolling around looking for action. Knowing what I know, I could see these girls heading for trouble.

One such girl was this little hottie Asian girl.

Just out of high school.

THE MALL RAT

This job at the mall was her first taste of freedom.

And she was interpreting that to mean going around the mall and being very aggressive, very obvious, coming on strong.

Whatever her job was, it seemed to entail walking around the back hallway a lot. She'd follow me, talk, flirt.

I wanted nothing to do with this girl. I noted that she was really heading for trouble. One day you may have to back up your "I'm a Big Girl" attitude. That attitude can get you into situations you don't want to be in. Be careful. You're not an old pro, you're a curious, horny teenager.

And the inevitable happens.

She walks into the food court one day with a friend. Her whole demeanour has changed.

A quick glance at her lower regions, superimposed on my catalogic memory of any good-looking woman, tells me she's been date-raped or something.

And it's bad.

I name this condition, "Slut Strut."

This results when a female of small proportions encounters a male or males of much larger proportions. The resulting difference in sizes eventually causes a space to develop between the woman's legs. Sometimes bow-leggedness as well.

And this is the worst case I've ever seen!

Her organs have literally been rearranged!

You can tell she's hurting. She looks emotionally fried.

As she walks away you can see the damage. You could see it coming. Patrolling around and acting trashy with some attitude ended in a way she never imagined. Maybe this was her first time, who knows?

So she met Brad, who took her to his pad. At home was Chad. But Brad was bad and Chad's a cad. Smoke, drink, getting rad. Brad and Chad want to be your Dad. It's all a fad. Here comes Tad. Let's all go mad. We're bad, bad, bad.

Now this girl is very sad!

Either wearing pants is too painful, or someone politely informs her that she now has "The Strut," because she now wears "Recovery Pants." These are large billowy pants.

Her patrolling days are over. She disappears soon after. The end of the innocence.

Don't get me wrong, but you be the judge.

Another girl was similar.
She was a bona fide creep, though.
Every time she entered the food court she'd glue her eyeballs to me.
But she was young, probably 18, Asian of some kind and hormonally challenged. She looked either Filipino, Japanese or some mixture. Pretty. Exotic. Steely, penetrating looks.
But eventually I crossed her path. I decided to go on a beer run one sunny afternoon. Out the doors, and down the sidewalk.
On that side of the mall there are park benches on small embankments, raised from the sidewalk.
And she's sitting on one of them, chatting away on her phone on this sunny day.
I walk past.
And she does it.
Admittedly, I'm not very nice. I do look.
But she's worse.
She spreads her legs and smiles at me.
She has no underwear on!
Need I go on.

But I did like the flashers. Another girl could tilt her body at an angle where I was "forced" to look into her braless shirt. If I moved, she moved. Like a dance. The last time I saw her, her irate boyfriend was pulling her away from Billy's! This one was a secretary at an office where I did business.
Flashers were cool.

Another group, although slightly less cool, were women who brought a friend, or a boyfriend into the action.
After awhile you are used to a wide range of occurrences, and this one was dubbed "The Bullshit Boyfriend Angle." In short, a "BBA."
On many levels, this is ill-advised. At the same time, some of these incidents would be quite humorous. And you'd learn a lot about "this woman." What is going on in there.

My attitude was always the same. I'm paying rent. This is a business and I have to be here. If you want to come here, I can't stop you. If you want to bring someone, it's a free world.

But whatever drama is in your head is yours alone.

I don't know you, never as much as asked you out, or even your name. Don't want to either.

There's now 3 in your picture, and you know 3's a crowd!

So I see the guy as the "goat," and the not so desirable traits of Little Miss Schemer!

As long as you maintain your totally innocent "I'm a Happy Fishman" stance, you'll come out unscathed.

"Psycho-Chick" always comes to mind here.

Tall, 20, natural blond. No fancy clothes. No make-up. Didn't need it.

She'd wheel past me in the middle of the afternoon for some reason.

And give me this huge range of looks and emotions. Very much a "I'm Equal to You Buddy Boy" kind of competitive mind set.

And she walked fast.

And glared hard.

In any list, she'd always be considered in the crazy category.

We never exchanged one word with her. And one night she turns up. With her boyfriend. They sit on the stools across from us.

I'm working with Stan.

I have no idea what Psycho-Chick said to him beforehand, or what she's saying to him now.

Remember, we've never said anything to each other.

And now the boyfriend is cursing us out, but we can't hear his threats. He's pissed. Fist into palm. He's a real bad-ass. Watch out.

She's hovering over him, saying things. Like gas on fire.

Stan doesn't know what's going on. He can't understand the behaviour and thinks it's extremely funny.

I enlighten Stan a little. And the boyfriend's not giving up.

We go about our work, and they finally slither off. I think the boyfriend gave us the finger as they left.

I don't know what she accomplished here. I guess that's why she's Psycho-Chick.

The rule was simply to act nonchalant, as if to act like these are faces in the crowd. Stand your ground. Who me?

One variety of stalker that brought up the "Theory of Unintended Consequences" was The Single Mom. You never know the unforeseen.
There are lots of hot single moms, and married ones too, and I love 'em all to death and all that…but…
There's one tiny problem.
Because they are single moms, they usually have kids in tow.
Hey I love kids, they're fun.
But they play into this.
From my observation, women won't be too forward if there are male children around.
But if they're with their daughters they're a "little" less inhibited. Could be a "girl thing" or "my ex is evil thing" or whatever. Who knows.
And now you're in a really bad position.
Why?
Because their now scheduled visits are accompanied by a "Are you going to marry my mommy?" look from some teeny girl.
How am I in this position?
Woe be it if the daughter is a teenager and starts to bring little hordes of giggly girls around.
I can handle lots of things.
I can handle the ghost.
I can handle being burned by hot grease.
I can handle lousy employees who ask me if Homer Simpson is still alive.
I can handle a lot of things.
But I can't handle this!
I can't.
It's sick.
I don't know why, but it's sick.
I just don't want to be in this position.

The worst case of this was a woman I called Julie.
Dark skinned. Some black or Spanish blood in there somewhere. Beautiful eyes. She worked at some outside job, maybe landscaping. So she was in great shape. No flies on her.

But here comes the baggage.
A teenage daughter.
And she toted the boyfriend along too! (The mother I mean!)
The way eye contact works is that really only the two participants know what's going on.
A third party may not even know what's going on. That's why movies are so great. You can watch the scene unfolding, and the eyes and face, straight on, are so much of it.
So the boyfriend is oblivious.
Real nice guy. Quiet. Respectful. Wanted to make them his little family. A guy working at a fish-n-chips shop could have told you different!
This woman thought this guy wasn't good enough for her. Neither smart enough nor rich enough is my guess.
He probably wasn't aware of it.
Week in, week out. Friday at 6 they'd arrive.
And the teenage daughter's looks intensified.
It was just so uncomfortable to be around these three and their thoughts.
No one's breaking any laws, but I wonder why you're wasting this man's time. You won't even let him buy you dinner!
As I said, nice enough guy.
Eventually, he disappears and it's just mom and daughter.
Of course they get worse.
No boyfriend to hold you back now!
These two are around right to our unhappy ending, but like everyone else they'll turn up one day and the stall will be boarded up. Or a new business will be going.
They're 2 of hundreds of customers who'll do that double-take.
At least I won't have to face starry-eyed teenage girls with their moms anymore.

But one girl could actually crack me, and make me run out of the place! Her name was "Miss July."
Tall slim, 20-21, pretty, legs to die for!
I believe the word for Miss July was "forward."
Indeed she was.
She ate in the food court a lot. And Billy's if she were there for lunch. Actually just a little after.

She'd talk to you from the cash register to the counter.

Then it would begin.

Four minutes of what amounted to a modeling assignment/Playboy photo shoot.

With clothes on.

Even clothed, this girl was provocative.

And suggestive. And worse.

Four minutes is a long time.

And then one day Miss July had an idea.

She overheard us telling a customer they had to wait 7 minutes for chicken instead of the customary 4 for fish.

So from that day on Miss July ordered a Cajun chicken salad.

She loved them, she said.

And so the show changed to 7 minutes. But one day I saw her coming into the food court, and for whatever reason, I cracked.

Yes, I admit it!

I cracked.

I couldn't take another "matinee" today.

I told Lyle to take over and I split.

I went out to the smoking area and had a smoke.

I made sure a full 10 minutes had elapsed and I went back in.

As I'm closing the door Lyle greets me with a smile.

I interpret the smile to mean that she's been and gone.

As I walk past Lyle, I see Miss July!

"She hasn't even ordered yet," Lyle smiles. Miss July is standing with her hands on her hips and has this, "You Bad Boy, I'll have to spank you later" look on her face.

"I'll have a Cajun chicken salad," she purred.

I just couldn't win!

Luckily, she spent too much time thinking about men and not enough time doing her job, and she got canned in less than 2 months.

But it was a long stretch. She was one of the most determined women I've ever met!

Up to now you'd think all stalkers were negative.

I only remember the funny and remarkable.

THE MALL RAT

As they go zipping through my head, I'd guess 6 or 7 of them were actually nice women. I probably missed out on something there.

Some of the highest compliments you can receive are from their interest in you.

We'll call these women "Women of Interest" rather than "Stalkers." "Stalker" has such ugly connotations!

They're not as forward. A little classier, so to speak.

While it's true they are a little more interested than they should be, you don't mind.

If I had to pick out the best looking woman I ever saw in the mall, it was a "Woman of Interest." Out of them all.

She worked in a clothing store, mostly on the weekends. Probably Filipino/Chinese, 20-21. This girl could pass any looks scorecard, 98 points out of 100.

I sold her food a number of times, but she loved quick food, particularly at the neighbouring A&W.

And she'd sit on the stools across from us. And eat. And stare.

If you ever wanted to run off and join the circus, this would be it!

But one Sunday morning she paid me the highest compliment.

It was early, 10 maybe. The food court was still dark. Only the lights from businesses open to serve breakfast, or a few of us there early.

I saw her round the corner by the Italian place.

It's 10.

She's going to grab an egg-whatever at A&W and head to the store.

I hate Sunday mornings. I'm always behind and never get ready on time. I'd sooner be watching news programs on the couch.

So I'm not really in the mood to go another round with her, no matter how nice she is.

If I do some work in the back room, the worst that can happen is she looks back on her walk away. 4 seconds at most.

It's too early for this, so I elect to prepare some fish in the back!

But I wander out to the drink area to count something. There's still a concrete wall between us.

Just at the second I bent over to do something, she peered around the corner.

Our faces were 2 feet apart, at the same height. Tete-a-tete!

She had no idea I was there.

She flushed red and started to babble.
I was in shock.
I'm glad she attempted to talk, because I couldn't!
She gaped around the corner on her own accord, and got her money's worth.
This was only a part-time job, and she faded away eventually.

But, like I say, it wasn't all bad.
Probably a good place to end.
A high note!

How Did I Get Here?

Every once in awhile a little rain must fall.
To this day, and for eternity, I will never understand the following chain of events.
How can one seemingly innocent action end up causing so much trouble?
How can I have so much bad luck?

Sometimes this mall is pretty empty.
Sometimes there are only four or five customers in the whole place. Some of the evenings can be slow . . . time of year, weather, sports . . . whatever.
I'm working with Stan.
At least he's fun. He's nuts to begin with.
It's one of those nights where you have pretty much everything done, and it's painful! You even have time to stand at the counter and do some people-watching.
Except that there aren't too many specimens to observe.
And the ones you are observing are buying grub from someone else.
I loathe those damn Greeks, they always get all the customers!
Billy's is one of the ultra-dead places on a slow night.

Some girl pulls up to the Taco place.
Average-looking.
I'm just looking around as usual, and her looks don't attract me at all.
But she's interested in me.
She starts doing this kind of stripper intro, and starts giving me this heavy eye contact.
She's now doing more suggestive little dance moves.
She's quite an artist. Maybe this is part of a "Dancing in the Streets" video.
Anyway, I'm trying to "kind of" ignore her. This is a little much.
But that's not really working.
She's getting right into it.

By chance, these are the slowest taco toilers on the planet.

They're a real trip.
Absolutely no connection whatsoever to the food they're making.
And it shows.
They handle the stuff like it's radioactive material.
Everything looks the same.
Their taco beef is something else.
You literally feel it cruising through your system.
And at night the owner has these lazy, rich Korean kids running the place.
One night a friend of theirs, emerged from the hallway with a tray of tacos, 15 or so.
And a three minute order typically takes 10.

So this chick has lots of time to "audition" for me.
She's a freak.
But probably a smart one.
If you are only average-looking, and a freak, throw yourself at people. The odds are probably o.k. on this sort of activity.
That's about the only rationale I can come up with on her.

Never one to hog the fun, I leave to go to the back and invite Stan to come up to the front.

I make some small talk with Stan, just two workies talking about nothing.
And she carries right on.
Stan can really get into this.
I really can't imagine doing this.
You are unbalanced, my Dancing Queen!
Or high.
Or both.
At this point, I feel the need to have some fun with Stan, so I ask him which one of us he thinks she's interested in.
Stan answers Stan.
I play shocked.
"No, of course it's me. I saw her first."
The good thing about Stan is that he believes himself, so you can go along with this line of conversation for a bit.
"She means the world to me."
She eats her food right across from us.
And she still has her weird fixation thing going on.
And now she is finished her food.
And she's gone.
What a weirdo.

Time to change tracks with Stan.
"Actually, you can have her, she was fat and ugly."
"No, no, you saw her first."
"No, no, I could never come between you two."
And so on. Typical mean, male appraisal.
I'm right in my element.
Stan knows he can't win.
And now we have to discontinue this kind of stupid conversation about our
little muse, as I have to leave for a few minutes to go do something.
As I'm leaving the back door, Stan and I are still taking parting shots at each other.
"No, your love for her is an inspiration. Good luck to you both."
"No, asshole, you take her."
"I know you love her. Good luck."

As I'm smirking into the hall a Starbucks girl is about to go up the ramp with the garbage can.

I'm in such a good mood I offer to assist this tub of lard who can't possibly push this up the ramp.

Stan and I continue our rather juvenile conversation.

I've done my good deed for the day and off I go.

Upon my return, I notice the mall security guard talking to the guy at the Greek place.

Now he's entering the place.

Now he's coming out.

Now he's going to the coffee shop.

Poking his head in the back.

Next place. Same thing.

And so on.

Now he's at our place.

"What's up?"

I forget his exact words, but there are madmen on the loose and threatening women, and so on, and they're maybe hiding in one of the food stalls.

This is the dumbest thing I've ever heard in my whole life!

Madmen on the loose? Who called this one in? You're obviously the victim of a prank.

The funniest thing is, since he knows us, he doesn't want to check our place.

And he continues on.

Checking.

Checking.

Then he's gone.

I can't really imagine this one.

"Hi, can I help you?"

"Yes, I'm a madman, and I was wondering if I could possibly hide in your place for awhile?"

"Sure. Not a problem. Fix yourself a snack."

"You're sure I'm no problem?"

"I'm not batting an eye."

I laugh to myself.

THE MALL RAT

This is all of a sudden becoming a very entertaining evening. Our Private Dancer. And now Dirty Harry. You never know.

All of a sudden the security guy is back.

He's gone to check out the complainant.

The complainant is a girl who works at Starbucks!

Apparently, two hoodlums from Billy's verbally abused her and they were threatening her! They had on red t-shirts!

I look at our shirts. I want to cry.

But I also want to stay ahead of this impending PR disaster!

So I quickly deduce that this attention-starved hippo turned drama queen took Stan and I's, "You can have her" conversation to mean we were talking about her!

I even helped the bitch!

I can't believe it.

Oh, merciful God, get me out of this one!

My brain lurches ahead. I see the upcoming security report! I have to head this off.

So I try to make this out to be one big, golly, gee-whiz misunderstanding. Oh my goodness!

See, we didn't even know what you were talking about when you first came around, and we were talking about a friend of ours, and it was in a slightly nicer way than we were portrayed, and you can see it's all one big over and done with nothing.

How can I make this person take no action?

Don't go back to Starbucks.

Don't file some dumb report.

Don't give it another thought.

The truth is, I know I can't.

Dancer + Tubby + Security Guard = Doom

He leaves.

In the direction of Starbucks.

I'm screwed.

Fatty will really run with it.

Her manager will be notified. A security report will be filed.

Mall Management read these like a tabloid. You don't want this at any cost.

But I have no way of verifying whatever damage has been done.
I don't hear a sound.
So I do a bit of a "recon" mission.
I just walk by Starbucks a few mornings in my street clothes, minding my own business.
They're busy at this time of day so it's fairly normal in terms of blending in.
I quickly get my answer.
All the employees eye me suspiciously. Dirty looks.
The odd one doesn't, but I quickly establish that the main staff does.
Later I hear from an employee of another shop that Starbuck's new rule is to have two employees do the garbage to be secure against the bad boys at Billy's!
That is total crap.

And you will never hear from the mall.
If they contact you, you may rebut some or all of the facts.
The people who read these reports already have the "truth" in their hands, so they don't want to listen to you at all.
I get ill thinking about this.
In particular, the Marketing Lady and her underlings come to mind.
A perfect crazy complaint.
And she didn't even have to do a thing.
She must have laughed when she read this one. Then copied it and put it in her "special file."
I must give her her due. I bow to you, but remind you that your easy pickings were merely dumb luck. Nevertheless, touché.
So this is what can happen when a combination of comedic happenchances collide . . . a chick who wants to nail you becomes a nail in your coffin.
I still can't believe it. To this day.
Anyway, hope your luck is better than mine. Remember this one. Wish I could forget it.

The Good Samaritan

Once in a while something nice happened.

Most of your customers were genuinely decent people going about their daily business.

I made friends with some great people who'd done interesting things in their lives.

One man I knew for awhile was at D-Day. Rushing the beaches. Went on to a successful career in oil. He gave me a ceramic bird as a gift when he was cleaning out his office. The bird had kind of a nautical theme and kids loved it. He was 92 or 93 at the time and was terminally ill. What a nice old guy.

He eventually died and his widow came around one day for a chat. She thanked me for being so kind and respectful to her husband. But the pleasure was all mine. I enjoyed his acquaintance.

You meet all kinds of people.

I noticed a small "SAS" tattooed on one man's wrist.

Then I noticed half of one finger missing.

At his age he would have been in the SAS in its infancy. This elite unit of the British Army was born in the jungles of Asia.

This guy has been in some sticky situations. I'm talking to a real-life Indiana Jones.

The SAS is actually one of the fighting forces you don't want to face in combat.
And this guy has seen some pretty heavy stuff.
I enquire about his membership in the SAS and about his finger.
He tells me I don't want to hear about the finger story.
Totally cool old guy. I love him.

Lots of regulars and you chat about whatever.
I loved this old lady we called "Granny."
Old and ornery, in a sweet way.
Born during the Depression, we tailor-made whatever she ordered so that nothing got wasted. Half the fries. Light on this. Whatever.
She liked to order you around a bit to assert her seniority.
And she'd bring her friend along. We'd split the order and nothing got wasted.
I liked regular customers because you wouldn't have to do much thinking.
Everyone knows the deal.

And Granny's here again today.
I even call her "Granny" by this time.
She orders food for a couple of people.
And a young woman walks up and stands next to "Granny."
"I'll pay."
"You don't need to, dear."
"No, I'll pay."
She hands me the money.
I'm thinking this is a niece or grand-daughter.
And I'm also thinking how nice it is that this young adult is actually paying for something.
In five years, if I've seen one trend, it's the "moochy child syndrome." People in their fifty's and sixty's still expecting Mom and Dad to pay for everything!
They even shy away when payment is due. It's so obvious.

THE MALL RAT

But here's a fine young lady.
Buying Granny some lunch.
The young lady disappears and I'm talking to Granny while the food is being prepared.
"Is she your grand-daughter?"
"What do you mean? I don't know her."
"She just bought you lunch."
"Never saw her before now."
I'm thinking Granny's prescription needs to be adjusted, and I don't pursue it.
There's obviously some confusion in Granny's mind.
I give her the food and off she goes.
I don't see the young lady around. Maybe she's gone shopping in the mall while Granny and friends eat. Then they leave.

About two hours later I see the young lady walking past Billy's.
I summon her over, perhaps I'm slightly concerned about Granny's well-being.
"She says she didn't know you."
"Oh. I don't know her."
"What do you mean? You paid for her lunch."
"Yeah I did. If someone can do something nice for my mother on the east coast, then I can do something nice for someone here today."
We talk for a minute or two and then she leaves.

A person performing Random Acts of Kindness.
We probably need a little more of that in the world.

Color Blind

I once worked with a girl overseas. A Chinese-American girl.
She was a work colleague, then a business partner.
The business partner part was a bad idea.
No. It was a good idea.
We made lots of money.
But it was rough going.

You see, she was really in the country to find a husband.
And she was a one-dimensional person.
Inside the classroom, she was Confucius, Ali, and Hitler all in one. I've never seen a teacher with such a hold on her students!
And parents.
And our business grew.
We started our school, by the way, by stealing 150 students from an English school that she was promoted to manage!
A really ethical move!
Twenty-four months later, she was burned out. No time to find a husband, so she melted down and returned to the States.
The guy who we stole the students from sued her for 150 K.

The judgement was eventually about 35 K.
We paid about a grand before she left the country. Absconded.
It was the last straw for her.
And she honestly thought she was innocent!
I have tons of stories about her and this English school, but suffice it to say I spent hundreds of hours around this person talking about nothing.
And talking about nothing with a girl looking for a husband entails mindless gabbing about relationships, expectations of people, and endless subjects involving the finer points of trying to figure out some way to make some guy like you. Thinking about this "slice of life" tires my weak male brain.

And one day she was telling me stories about a guy she knew in high school.
His nickname was "Yellow Fever."
He was apparently a white kid programmed for Asian girls.
Her stories centered around his constant presence and hitting on new, unsuspecting Asian students.
Fetishes!
I once knew a guy who loved overweight women. We called him the "Meat Man." He was a real dragon slayer.

I'm not sure if "Black Plague" replaces "Yellow Fever" but our mall was graced with a young lady of similar bent.
Meet "Big Red."
She was in her early 20's.
Red hair. Light. Long.
Freckles. Of course.
Tall.
Not bad looking, but I'm not a red-hair type of person.
She had a cute face, and her dirty thoughts would find themselves on display there.
I'm not sure of her lineage. Could be Irish, Dutch or any of the Scandinavian ones.
Hard to say.

And Big Red worked at what I call a trinket/junk shop on an island stall in a main hallway. Selling silver jewellery and stuff like that.

This kind of island stall is just the best for traffic flow and people watching. There are people coming at you every moment of the day.

And Big Red had a little fetish.

Black guys.

In the presence of a black male she was right in her element. Bubbly. Obvious. The only thought going through their heads was questioning how lucky they were to become.

Or not.

Don't worry about the "Or Not."

You are "in like Flynn."

And this is not a particularly black city.

Or a black part of town.

A mall's a mall's a mall.

So you don't see too many black people around.

They don't eat fish-n-chips anyway.

Que sera sera.

So it makes it all the more noticeable.

If you're walking past their island, the only customers she'll be yakking with are black males.

And she's animated.

It's her "sales pitch."

Whatever, the chemical arrangement of her brain is, this is her high.

The brain made some kind of favorable connection, and that's it.

I don't think she likes white guys at all.

At least not me.

I've seen her around forever practicing her shtick, so she always gives me a hateful or non-existent look. It's as if to say that she knows what I think of her cause I've seen her over and over, and I'm irrelevant anyway.

That's true.

But I'm not really judging you, anyway.

I don't really care.

I honestly don't.

That's your thing.
Go for it.

And she does.
Like Mr. Yellow Fever, she's not big on things like preferences, likes, dislikes. Details.
One Criteria Only.
Are you black?
And she's shameless.
No Don Kings, but there are a few Fridge Perrys.
And a Michael Jackson.
In the Jackson Five Era!
Like 16.
She's even buying him an after-school snack.
She's literally 9 inches away from him as he eats, with her angle adjusted so he can look down her dress as he eats.
He's going to have an interesting day!
It's going to be one of those days where you learn more in the playground than the classroom!
And because he's so young, she's really putting it on.
Out of embarrassment?
Or because he's just told her his parents are out of town for a few days?
I can barely watch this round.

But that's Big Red.
It's a kind of a "Food for _____ Program."
Luckily, she doesn't work for the U.N.
I can see some bureaucrat in New York scratching his head.
"Hmm. How can this be? The latest data on Africa says the birth rate is zero, but STD's are up 25 billion percentage! Hmm. And we only added 1 "AID(s)" worker, that girl, Big Red, I believe her name was. Hmm. What does it all mean?"

She's a real go-getter.
But one day she's gone.

Some people you notice when they're gone.
And besides, you never see her at the trinket shop.
Maybe she's gone off to marry a soccer team in Kenya? Who knows?
Anyway, I don't see her around any more.

The cast at the mall is always changing and at some point in time later on we get a new maintenance supervisor (writing this first draft, I mistakenly wrote "survivor." A slip of some kind!) They're usually "recovering" from something, and have strange extended families.
They're usually female, 60-ish, and gripe a lot.
But this one's different.
He's Jamaican or something. About 25.
He's a hoot.
Totally out of place.
This guy didn't come all this way to wear some goofy cleaning company shirt with his name embroidered on it!
You can tell he thinks this whole deal sucks.
And it does suck.
He's basically herding a bunch of Philippino senior citizens, trying in vain to get this crew to clean things somewhat properly.
Anyway, he doesn't care much for this aspect of the job, so he starts disappearing more and more. He gets pretty comfortable with his work evasion plans, and starts making what look to be "guest appearances."
But he's around somewhere.
He's like a kid in a candy shop. This mall is filled with women. You can talk to people all day.
I see him hustling the odd woman.
I never see him doing much work.

At the same time this opportunity isn't being utilized to the fullest, in his estimation.
Look at all these women.
But look at me in this goofy sanitation uniform.
It's hard to convince these women of my extraordinary desirability while dressed in this get up.
"Oh yeah, baby. My Benz is outside. Let's go to my penthouse crib. The

clothes? Don't worry, I'm shootin' a video."

She'll soon discover the Benz is a bus, the crib is a basement apartment, and the only video that is going to be made with a cell phone!

Alternatively, he could try to convince women that he's really a bigshot, doing this for other reasons.

This will be a bit of a hard sell as well.

It's the uniform.

And then he has a flash of genius.

I gotta hand it to this guy.

He finds his way out.

That's right. Take your biggest vulnerability and turn it upside down.

He heads to a 2-for-1 suit sale, and transforms himself into "Pimp Daddy."

The higher-ups can't say much. He's in a suit. Business-like.

And now he's not visibly identified with this cleaning company.

He can be in the mall as The Player, not as The Cleaner.

It's brilliant.

His self-esteem improves. He even develops his own little strut. Sherman Helmsley-like.

Too bad his "posse" consists of seniors who can't speak English. I don't think we have a Beyonce or J-Lo, but we have a Circumcision, and Incarnation, and a Clementia. She's the best, only talks to objects, not people.

His "Homies" are Vic, who likes to stare at men urinating in the bathrooms, and "Dip," who actually dips when he walks. His name is actually Dip, folks. I'm not making anything up.

Actually, this collection would make a rather interesting video.

I see him even less in the food court, and occasionally hitting on some chick.

He even starts to sport a fedora!

It's a little much.

But hey, it beats his previous uniform.

I really admire this. I really do. Nothing better than someone who can solve a problem.

And one day "Big Red" reappears.
Oh, it's been a good 6 or 8 months.
She's over talking to the staff at one of the food stalls. A visit.
Smiling away.
And I think if only "those 2" knew each other. Too bad.
And then Pimp Daddy appears from the other side of the food court.
Dressed to the Nines.
And he walks past me.
Then stops.
Then heads up the other line.
Why?
Because he knows someone.
Guess who?
And they're old buddies!
Seriously, she probably hasn't been in the mall half an hour.
And they're talking like they're making plans.
A "See You After Work" kind of conversation.
And she gives him a coy but dirty kind of look.
She hasn't changed a bit.
And the funny part is that I never see either of them ever again. Ever!!!!
He must have quit his job and was just back to get something.
Or they transferred him to the Playboy Mansion.
Alas, we'll never know.
Once their paths crossed…love is blind.
At least color blind.

Who Ya Gonna Call?

Something very bad must have happened here.
Was there an old west gun fight here and the Snake-Eye Kid met his end? Or is this place built on some burial grounds?
I've seen ambulances leave the mall. Maybe the occupant was already dead, and comes back to finish his or her shopping. Perish the thought. I don't like shopping very much.
About 10 years ago there was a drive-by and a young person died on the sidewalk.
And then there's the story of the escalator repairman who got ground-up working alone at night.
Who knows?

All I know is that Billy's was inhabited by a "GRADE A SPIRIT." It had its own personality, pranksterish and festive, no set patterns in its activities, and could exhibit emotions.
Oddly, and luckily, outside the circle of people who had interactions with "this thing," (we never named it), we never talked about it with "outsiders." It was our thing. It was almost a sense of empowerment to deal with something few get to deal with, but conceal this to most of the people you know and deal with. That's the "Oddly."

The "Luckily" is that there's no better way to extinguish whatever little credibility you have with someone than to start talking about "ghosts." It's true.

Here's the world as I now know it.
Ghosts, spirits, whatever do exist. This I know.
At the same time, the number of people who actually confront these energies are small in ratio to the population.
The manifestations of these ghosts are diverse.
Few ways to capture the images of what these ghosts are doing. Or why.
So our minds are not equipped to deal with information, second hand, that tells of things that our eyeballs have never seen.
We reject it.
Towards the end of our tenure, I did mention around one or two customers the existence of our ghost.
The reaction was the same.
Mentally, I went from "Ok Seafood Guy" to "Loony Seafood Guy" in a nanosecond.
Physically, people will recoil a little, their eyelids will flutter, and the look is "I Reject All Incoming Info." Period.

So luckily it was just a Billy's thing. I'd never even discuss it with employees who hadn't been around for one of the events. But if a person was around for one, they believed and understood more of the others.
So I fully understand why people don't believe in ghosts. I've never seen a U.F.O. I can understand the nature of U.F.O.'s, but I'm not 100% convinced. And they're fairly easy to visualize in one's mind.
Ghosts are not. They're diverse. Shows like "Paranormal" go some way to measure and explore and capture this world. I can actually understand some of what the case studies in this program are talking about, but I'll explain that later.
But I do fully understand "sceptics," in any line of thought. Any.
In the post-Billy's era I have no more or no less interest in ghosts. I think my brain realizes that the randomness of such activity is thus that spending time studying it is largely futile. If there's an interesting ghost show on T.V. I may watch it. But that's about it. Billy's was Billy's, leave it there, but note

that pertaining to that little sliver of earthly happenings, you know what you know. That's it!

Prior to Billy's, I had one brush with the paranormal.

It was many years ago.

I was working very late one night in a very old warehouse. A 100 year-old warehouse. My family owed it.

I worked there from boyhood. During my later years, my friends and I would occasionally use the place as a late night watering hole. It was near the bar district.

It's about midnight. It's way later than closing time, but I rarely stay past 2 or 3. So it's about midnight.

I'm on the third floor. I'm straightening out some stock for a sale. This building was very well-built and is silent.

But now I'm hearing someone walking around on the fourth floor, over my head. These are footsteps. Taken deliberately. Sequential.

My adrenalin pumps. Oh yeah. Big time.

This is a break-in. (Never mind that I didn't hear this "break-in," or anything else until the footsteps! But your mind is only reacting at these times.)

We have been broken into before, so this is my first inclination.

Well, I don't have much of a choice.

I grab a piece of wood and proceed up the stairs. Into the dark rooms. I don't know whether to make noise or not!

I'm running on all cylinders!

I investigate each room.

No one.

Nothing.

Now this really frightens me.

I kind of cease working for the night and get on home.

The next morning my father reveals that this was probably my great-great grandmother, who started our business. My father hadn't had any interaction with her, but other people had seen and heard her. He also informed me that this was the end of the subject.

OK.

So I had one brush with this before Billy's. That experience didn't make me more or less interested in this subject. It's so random that you shouldn't think too much about it. But note it. It is strange. And note the adrenalin rush. Part of you wants a repeat performance. It never comes.

But Billy's was a bit different.

The origin of our ghost was unknown.

It came.

It went

It did different things.

It may have been different spirits. We may have been a spiritual bus stop!

But the main collective trait was longevity.

Start to finish.

It would go on holiday, but then new things would happen.

And this is the answer to why we would never do anything about it. (Even if we could.)

I did try a Sylvia Browne "get out of here" deal.

I think I hurt his feelings!

The adrenalin rush and childlike sense of amazement was worth it all. After the period of shock had worn off, I was enthralled with what had happened! Lyle and I used to joke that we'd leave when the knives came out of the knife block and flew at our heads! It was part joke, part verbalization of our fear, and part warning to our guest!

Now, "feeling" a ghost or spirit is one thing, physical evidence is another.

I see how people can "feel" a spirit, but to a second or third party that is impossible to visualize or understand. Even the person "feeling" this should have doubts.

So in dealing with our apparent guest spirit, I always applied the following: Try to explain this event any other way possible. When you have run way out of the plausible, accept it. Marvel at it. Laugh at it even.

But try to explain it any other way first.

Electrical surges. Electrical shut-offs. Practical jokes. Emergency or security personnel in here after hours. Seismic activity. Wind. Thieving employees. Anything.

Your mind is always attaching a betting odds to each theory, them deciding not to go to the betting window. New and even more far-fetched scenarios cross your mind.

And these are just for the occurrences that you "find."

THE MALL RAT

The ones you "see," firsthand, really test your mind.

Lyle and I became quite sleuth-like in trying to explain away this or that. We must have sounded loony, with our zany theories of how things move.

But you have to think like that, because the occurrences observed had just defied everything you know as "normal."

So it's a bit of a process.

And I'll admit a process in itself just accepting this state of things!

These are my basic thoughts and opinions about ghostly matters.

Yes, they exist. But don't sweat it.

In the first period I owned Billy's I didn't give it much, if any, thought. As I make clear, I have no real interest in ghosts.

But from the beginning, I notice a certain oppressiveness in the air there. Particularly in the back room.

This may be attributed to the small space that it was, but the feeling was just different. It was as if something was exerting mild pressure on you. The room felt full when you were the only one in it.

But this would come and go.

Frankly, I was too busy learning how to run this crazy seafood place to notice things.

But what I started to notice were missing pots, pans, and other small pieces of restaurant equipment.

What would you think?

Exactly.

The employees.

These are young fellas who are starting their own apartments.

So they lifted some of my crappy stuff.

Whatever.

You're so busy running things, and this is small stuff anyway.

It's time for Nat to move on. Nathan's been an OK employee. One day he was so high at work he thought our logo was talking to him.

Nat needs more pay than Billy's can provide, so he quits in an organized, civil way.

But I'm adamant about getting my uniforms back before I pay him.

This results in some shuttle diplomacy which ends over a beer at his apartment.

This is a drug house. Cops are over at a neighbor's house. And everyone's relieved!

This is when I learn that they stole food from me, but not the stuff I thought they stole!

They even said my stuff wasn't really good enough for them to steal!

At this point, I'm having serious questions about Billy's security, and a few days later I speak to Lyle about this.

After we discard theories about staff honesty, Lyle tells me this has been going on since he's been here, but didn't want to broach the subject with me because he liked working here and didn't want to come off sounding loony.

Well, he may have something there, because some of it would really test my "why?" skills! Something semi-important left in a certain place the night before, now gone. It may be as simple as a pot you left on the counter, and is now gone. Vanished. It is no longer here.

So I'm definitely thinking that there is something going on here.

Lyle and I also both share another occurrence that adds credence to the presence of something other-worldly.

He seems to see a figure jumping or darting, out of the corner of his eye. More commonly, he will see a figure darting away in the reflection in the glass doors in the big cooler in the back room. This cooler has long glass doors and is situated half-way along the wall, acting as a kind of mirror on the whole room. On the near side of the room, the freezer impedes your vision from door to door.

And I know exactly what he means.

There's not much we can do about it. It's kind of intriguing in a certain way.

Remember, anything that happens must be approached in a scientific way, if possible.

After exhausting all the theories, ease into the possibility that Mr. Ghost has been active. Go for any theory and it will soon not hold up.

On the whole the spirit interacted with Lyle more than myself.

I don't know how many times I'd turn around or bump into a flustered Lyle. The darting spirit vignette was always around him.

THE MALL RAT

He didn't spend all that much time there alone. I did.

The spirit interacted with 4 or 5 other people at Billy's, half of these I can attest to, as I was there for whatever happened.

As an aside, just for a moment think about the notion of this darting figure.

Saw it perhaps a 100 times to Lyle's 500.

When he would describe a variation of this, I knew exactly what he was talking about.

Now if I had to describe what I saw in picture perfect detail, I know I could never convey that image. Perfectly.

This is why most people don't believe in ghosts, or want to talk about them.

I understand perfectly.

I digress.

The first time I knew something was really wrong, when I surrendered to the existence of this spirit, was one morning when I entered the place.

I turned on the lights, put down my stuff, and all these appliances were plugged into different sockets from the normal ones.

Five or six in 2 or 3 plugs.

One of the hook-ups looked funny, kind of poltergeist-ish with its complexity.

It was just plain weird.

At this point, as with everything, you go through all possible scenarios.

There really are none.

There is no one who would have entered our place, and did this.

So I'm a believer now.

But throughout our encounters with this spirit, we seem to accept it, and never really talk about it too much, or to "outsiders."

It's pointless.

You can't really describe it.

It comes and goes. Maybe it's gone right now and never coming back. Who knows?

It just "is," and we take it or leave it.

But when it chooses to press your doorbell, it will.

In the same line of thinking as the disappearing pots, I thought one of my employees had stolen one of my Metallica CD's.

I knew it was him!

But I didn't say anything to him.

And I dumped the place upside down looking for it.

I could find a hair, let alone a CD case.

And then one morning it was laying on a piece of napkin on the back table!

This was a few months later! My suspect didn't work there anymore.

All throughout Billy's, I never thought for a moment that the spirit wasn't that of a young man, I always think 30's.

And I always settle on someone who passed on early, too early, and wanted to pursue some earthly endeavours before moving on.

And we had the perfect venue.

Our back room.

Best party in the mall.

No piped-in garbage music for us.

Zeppelin, Nirvana. Zevon. Lots of metal. Lots of classic.

Blasting.

The walls were 3 feet thick. I'd never seen anything like this. You could have the music absolutely blaring in our back room, and due to normal mall noise and the walls it only sounded like a far away radio at counter distance or in the hall.

Beautiful.

Happy Hour at 8. Or 7:30. OK it's only 7. One of my daily rituals was the run to the beer store. Faithfully.

Drink and clean up. Usually Lyle and I.

Our back room had a cool, dumpy nightclub effect, due to the fact that only half the lights worked.

The only times we'd even attempt to have them working was when we were expecting a health inspection.

We'd be literally blinded for a day or two!

Oh, right. Reg took it upon himself to fool with the bulbs one day and electrocuted himself. That was actually very funny.

THE MALL RAT

This spirit loved that kick-back Dropkick Murphy's ambiance. You were its ongoing hangout.

When we'd be blasting Deep Purple and gunning a few cheap ones, you'd feel way more presence in the room than the 2 or 3 of us.

The area near the stereo, the prep table along the back wall, sometimes seemed to have a lot of energy around it. Hovering.

Our spirit could even spark up the chronically depressed Brian.

He was blasting the Maiden one day, sitting on a milk crate eating lunch.

He was probably thinking about how shitty his life is, and so on.

Next thing I know he's running up to me, all animated. Excited.

As his mandible was moving, and he was contemplating the next horrific disaster of his life, a CD zoomed off the shelf, over his head!

He had adrenalin to burn.

I quickly grilled him on flight path and velocity.

This spirit always uses enough force to preclude other occurrences.

He means it.

He's in shock and recants the tale over and over. And then stands there. Forever.

Time to get back to work!

But I do interview him about his thoughts and feelings. I can see from his sense of marvel why I like this thing so much.

It's just this cool little show we get to see once in awhile!

One evening I was mopping my way out to leave.

I pushed the garbage can on wheels out to the front to give myself more room. I locked the door. The can had a fresh bag in it.

Mop. Leave by back door.

The next morning I come in. I turn on the lights. Normal stuff. I go to the front. Unlock the door and proceed.

Wait. My garbage can now has a sleeve of cups in it!

From the back room!

Separated by a wall and a locked door.

Answer?

There isn't one.

No one would go to the trouble of entering, procuring said cups, and placing them perfectly in the garbage can.

Even the present crop of security guards look so brain-dead that they couldn't possibly engineer this prank.

I liked the collective episodes, as it was fun to see other people's reactions.

On a busy lunch-hour, our friend chose to push/throw the prep table across the back room.

Lyle, Len and I were up front.

Our reactions were the same—count the live bodies, realize something is terribly wrong, and dart for the door way to see what is causing the 150-lb table to screech across the room.

What a rush!

The table legs leave a mark on the floor. This set was dark and wide. Noticeable.

No explanation held.

Even if you were the cat burglar of the century you couldn't get in, push the table, and exit in the split-second between sound and investigation.

Impossible.

I know the back door and "how it closes" better than anyone. Your brain would have to be unbelievably quick to pull off all the moves.

There was not a soul in the hallway, and you couldn't have moved to a hiding place in that much time.

Again, no rational person would do this.

But the collective adrenalin rush, the shared experience of something so weird was cool.

So different things would happen, all centered around the back room at Billy's. Coming and going. Certainly Lyle and I were well used to it, along with a smattering of others.

But what happens now speaks to the fact that although your brain is well used to the idea, sometimes even then you can't accept what happens. Seeing is indeed believing.

It's mid afternoon.

Lyle comes up to me.

Apparently, all the spoons have been dancing on the hooks on the side wall!

He re-enacts this for me.

Who should accept this more easily than I?

No one.

THE MALL RAT

I look at Lyle like he's mad.
I just can't exactly wrap my brain around this!

Then one Saturday morning, it happens to me!
Without question, this is the most frightening moment of my life. Well, almost.
Only it's not the spoons, it's the tongs.
It's 8:54.
I know that because in 60 seconds I'll be looking at the time wondering when Lyle will be turning up!
I'm putting fish away.
In front of me is the dividing wall with shelves. Shelves with supports. We use the supports to hang our tongs over. Tongs are essential to us and there are half a dozen pairs or so hanging there. Fourteen to sixteen inches from my face.
Then all of a sudden, they go berserk.
And not in any sort of rhythmic way.
Just berserk. Frantic.
I'll go with 10 to 15 seconds.
I'm frozen.
Then they stop.
Not in a nice sort of pendulum way. They just stop. Zero.
I've never seen anything like this before! Mr. Doubting Thomas is now in shock waiting Lyle to show up. I guess I'll survive 5 minutes!
That's a very rushy 5 minutes!
I Told You So Lyle is saying, "See. I told you so."
I wish everyone in the world could see this once. Our collective knowledge would be greater.
This is enough for me, though.
The adrenalin rush and sense of terror was as much as I could deal with.

A couple of staff members had slightly different manifestations of our spirit.
Lyle's brother, who would also see the cooler glass reflections, twice saw a mass of light slightly larger than myself following me around.
I experienced nothing like this, so I can't vouch for it.

To understand this subject matter you will always be "chasing ghosts!" You didn't see it and you'll never really comprehend it.

One of the ladies had a different experience altogether.
I was out getting ice from another place and when I returned to the counter she was frozen. Like my ice.
"I thought you were coming in the back door, and when I entered the back a huge rush of energy pushed me back out here."
I can sometimes feel a presence in that room, for sure, but it's never exerted any, real physical force on me. I can sort of see what she's getting at, but not entirely.
Her famous line to me on this episode was, "I don't know how you can be alone in here. I will never spend 1 minute in here alone again." Petrified.

Our little spirit was active right to the end.
On the T.V. show "Paranormal" they often call in Chip the Expert for his take on this energy or spirit. A lot of those are real bad ass spirits, so I don't envy him much.
But one thing Chip can do is tell the team and audience what the spirit is feeling or expressing.
I can see this. This is a form of channelling.
Most of the time, if I picked up any feeling, it was one of happiness, of someone experiencing a good time. It's a very funny feeling, hard to describe.
But on the day the property management company called and canned us, the feeling in the room was something else.
I'd been tipped off months in advance as to our demise, so I wasn't feeling particularly sad or remorseful.
But something in that room was.
Outside that room, no. Nothing.
Inside that room was like being in a funeral home to the power of ten. Dark. Sad.
And a lot of energy slightly pressing. Filling the room.

It was weird.

Because of the juvenile nature of the antics, I somehow picked up a feeling of condescension from the spirit.

It was as if to show you that even people as dumb as you can't miss this one.

And the final performances subtly illustrated that.

All down the line Lyle and I joked (meant) that we'd leave when the knives came off the wall.

They never did, so we were content with whatever entertainment was provided.

But in the final months I wanted to finish up a number of things.

One of them was to have Lyle work with me on a few Sundays.

Lyle hated Sundays.

He never worked them. This is how he lasted as an employee for so long. It was an unwritten rule.

But he'd do a few now. A bit of a walk down Memory Lane. Sundays were a drag, but the draggy customers could provide some memorable laughs.

It's about 4. We go at 5. We're cleaning up. And we're both in the back room, hovering around the prep table, talking about something.

At this point, a 3 foot steel rod, stored on top of the cooler, and used to dislodge things in the fryers, zooms between our heads, lands on the table, and hits the floor. Zoom. Zoom. Crash. Boom. Bang!!!!!

Our clever little fellow reduced himself to the thickness of a pancake and rammed his palm into the rod. If you want to look at it in human terms.

There's no explanation to be found.

We said knives. It says rod.

We said at our heads. It says between your heads.

Mr. Condescension.

It was definitely close enough to my head to cause a reflex reaction.

And it re-ran this episode as is final hurrah. In the last week.

I wasn't there.

This time it was Lyle and Sally.

Same scenario.

Five or six days to the end.

This one really was the final straw. Or rod.

Not for the rod sailing across the room, but for when Lyle informs me of this.

I'm at a Little League game.

Last game of the year. Winner take all. Championship game.

We're down 9-2 or something after 3, but manage a 9-9 tie after 6.

Extra innings.

My boy is up.

He's the winning run.

The other parents don't particularly like me, or my advice.

The bottom line is Little League pitching is at times not so hot, so getting hit is as good as a single.

He listens.

He gets hit.

Gets to second on a wild pitch.

And to third on another.

The pitcher is melting.

He's on third. None out.

It's very exciting. It's all on the line.

At the exact moment that the pitcher winds up, Lyle calls.

My son steals home on yet another wild pitch.

As he slides and everyone's waiting for the call, I have frantic Lyle on my cell, so the jumping spectators impair my vision.

He's safe. He's the hero!!

It's pandemonium, Little League style!

I didn't see it. I didn't see it!

I couldn't get rid of Lyle.

That lousy ghost just robbed me of one of those Great Parenting Moments!

I was furious.

We drove home happy. And angry.

The final days passed uneventfully.

If I did think about the spirit, it was to express anger. You idiot.

We're done.

As with many things in life, this was something that would eventually end.

That was that experience.

And it hasn't given me any reason to study ghosts or the supernatural. It's too random.

I can see why you don't believe in ghosts.

But you can see why I do.

P.S. The upshot from ghosts is that they present new problems and don't really solve anything. You have many new spiritual questions. There will be no answers.

Tell me the name of the next Kentucky Derby long-shot winner!

Tell me something of use.

I actually view this kind of thing as evidence of a Higher Being, as the Atheists and other Godless groups are diminished in my eyes.

As my version of the universe "expands," my monotheistic beliefs are only strengthened. The more complicated it gets, the more it points to the inevitable—ONE GOD.

No God at all? Impossible.

Polytheists? When was the last time a group agreed on anything? And how could multiple sources of power develop?

God doesn't share power. No can do.

Which isn't to say there isn't truth in all earnest religions. As long as the direction's right.

Things like ghosts make you think!

But there's only one questions that totally stumps me: How did God get to be God?

Think about it.

The Stoner Nation

Drugs.
The scourge of our era.
Part of our social history now.
In the 60's and 70's it was fun drugs. Weed and acid.
Sure, some people went off the rails, but the worst crime a stoner can commit is robbing a bag of cookies.
From the 80's on, the world of drugs gets meaner.
Coke. Crystal Meth. Crack. Ecstacy.
These are all nasty, downward-spiralling substances that society ingests in wholesale amounts.
It's crazy.

And every second ad on T.V. is for some kind of prescription drug.
I never knew there were so many illnesses!
I like the ads where they are trying to convince you that you're sick, and that this "condition" actually exists.
A nation of druggies.

Again, there are good drugs and bad drugs.

THE MALL RAT

It's sad to watch a teenager trying to restart their lives in a sandwich shop after a bout in rehab.

It's good to see them trying to turn their lives around, but ultimately they disappear quickly.

Usually due to discipline problems. Their brains are so fried that they have all kinds of imaginary conflicts with people.

One of the nearby coffee shops had a crackhead working the opening shift.

She worked there a long time and was formerly quite nice-looking.

Then the crack took over.

By the time she left she was a skeleton.

Sometimes I'd see her hunched down like a squirrel, leaning on the mall, smoking a cigarette on her break.

She looked like death.

So there are the drugs we must avoid.

I like those posters that show a crack head in 10 one-year interval pictures.

10 years to the grave.

Parents should put one up some place in the house!

Many of my employees were druggies.

One guy came to work on some kind of natural Indian drug. He was so high our company logo was talking to him. Good guy to have around hot fat!

Fani California has by now either gone to rehab or is in serious trouble.

But most of them were the happy, pot-smoking teenager types.

And many of the customers were as well.

Smoke a few, get the munchies, and head off to the food court.

One of my favorites were The Stoner Family.

Mr. and Mrs., and two teenage sons.

Totally blasted. But trying to act normal.

Nice folks.

They probably have a final smoke out in the parking lot, do a little shopping, then dig into the fish-n-chips.

It's funny watching stoned parents looking at stoned children.

I guess the family that bongs together, bonds together. Or the family that rolls together, holds together. Modern day values. It works.

"Dad, can I have a run to my dealer's house?"

"Sure, son. But don't forget to pick up some for your mother and I."

"Look. Just what I wanted for Christmas, new roach clips."

"Dad, have you been stealing out of my piggy bank again?"

"No, son. That was the tooth fairy."

But one thing you can say for druggies is that they're appreciative customers. They plow right into the plate.

Druggies can also ask some incredibly dumb questions.

One guy ordered halibut (filet) for himself, and calamari (rings) for his girlfriend.

Even if you are completely brain-dead you'd at least know what you ordered.

I bring out the tray.

Mr. Bloodshot Eyes looks at me and says, "Which one is which?"

I don't miss a beat. "How much weed have you smoked?"

He giggles and takes the tray away.

These are the harmless druggies.

But the crackheads can turn on a dime.

I used to go to a supermarket twice a week, early morning. To get things for Billy's.

One morning I notice this car driving next to me. If I speed up, so does he.

If I slow down, so does he.

It's like 7 am.

What's up with this guy?

About a mile down the road I have to stop at some traffic lights.

Mr. Crackhead pulls up next to me.

All of a sudden, tattoos, facial hair and dirty clothes are emerging out of the car with an awl in its hand!

That thing looks sharp!

Apparently I've slighted Mr. Crackhead in some way.

I "crack" the passenger's window about 2 inches so I can listen to his invitation to step out of the car so he can kill me!

In Asia you drive with a baseball bat in the back seat. It's almost mandatory. Too bad I don't have one now.

Oh well, the light turns green and I speed off. Left, right, left. No more Mr. Crackhead.

But this is how a simple act like going to the store can turn tragic. At 7 am.

This is the Stoner Nation.
At work. At play. En route.
Drugs are everywhere.
Don't do drugs.
Look at that 10-year poster.
It could be you.
You could walk up to me and say, "I'll have a Teen Burger." Burgers are next door.

Or worse, forget to speak.

Don't worry, we are able to understand "Drug-ese." It's like Handicap Access. Ya gotta have it.

It's the Stoner Nation.

Nice Recovery

The people I bought this business from gave me precious little advice on how to run it.

They were so glad to be rid of this star-crossed place that they went "semi-comatose," and got away at every opportunity! Zombie-like.

"Yul-learn" was the common answer to any query I had!

"And remember, there's always someone watching you," was the only other piece of advice she offered.

She even had this saying taped to the cash register with a grumpy-face drawing.

I promptly took it off the cash register at first opportunity. I hate clutter.

This lady looked like Harpo Marx, so watching her must have been something.

But she was right.

Your were on stage.

Your work area is open to the public's scrutiny.

One of my cooks would wipe his face with his forearm and sniffle every bloody time he put up an order.

Bon Appetit.

I think she spied on the staff a bit, sitting far away, and then turning up unexpectedly with a litany of wrongdoings. The staff did some rather hilarious imitations of her chastising them. She was a real hag.

Their other funny imitation was of the time they phoned the owners, who were apparently making love at the time of the call.

This one was pretty funny.

But when you think about it, someone is probably always watching you.

If someone asked me what are my 2 or 3 lasting memories of my years in Asia, I'd have to say one of them is that you could be in some obscure place at some ridiculous hour and there'd always be someone around.

You were never alone. Never.

Sometimes I'd be outside my house at 4 or 5 in the morning and there'd be people in nothing alleys, doing, well, nothing.

Walk under a bridge at 3:30 am.

Someone will be there.

It used to fry my brain.

And in the 9-11 era most big city centres have hundreds and hundreds of surveillance cameras installed to monitor every square inch of public space.

In England these cameras are very common.

Probably solves a lot of other crimes as well.

So we are being observed far more than we think. It's neither good nor bad if you're not up to anything.

It's fun to observe someone who doesn't think anyone is watching them.

They really believe no one is watching them. So you have a real honest look at them.

I once observed a very funny person in Germany.

This person was a real hoot. When someone does something totally unexpected, you just gotta laugh.

There's a very picturesque town in "Bavaria somewhere" called Rothenberg ob der Tauber.

As the name implies, it's set next to a river. A walled medieval gingerbread village.

Perfect in all respects, a famous wood-carver named Reumannsheider or something gave the town a few masterpieces. The coolest toy shops I've ever been in are in Rothenberg.

Nice place.

But it's very touristy.

And I want to experience it as quietly as possible, all to myself. I don't want to overhear other people's conversations, and I don't want to smell diesel from tour buses.

So I get up very early. Half hour after daybreak.

For some reason I like to go to places at that hour and grow into the light.

The coolest place to drive to in the middle of the night is the Grand Canyon. It's so huge even in the dark you can see it miles away!

What I want to do is walk along the medieval walls. They are 2 or 3 stories high. They must have had some pretty lame invaders, but I guess walls are walls.

It's a beautiful morning. Cool. No noise.

I'm up on the walls walking along, imagining defending this town from some barbaric tribe. I can't say I'd enjoy looking through these wall holes all day. Oh well, life was pretty simple back then, and this might have been classified as "interesting."

And now I see a woman on her bicycle.

She's 60, gray and blue plaid skirt, glasses, gray hair, but she's vigorous.

How European. Lady of the House peddling to a market somewhere.

Germans always have this air of respectability to them.

Now she's stopping.

And putting up her bike stand.

Wow, these Germans are so industrious, it looks like she's going to do a minor repair on the way to the market!

Well, not quite. Kinda.

She's standing and looking around.

It's a major street, but she's the only one on it.

And now she's squatting down, hiking up her skirt, and still looking around.

Now I see a river flowing across the pavement.

Origin appears to be from under this previously respectable woman's skirt.

Granny's having a leak!

And she's looking around like a burglar.

THE MALL RAT

It's hilarious.

Well, her bladder appears to be in order, or not, depending on how you look at it.

Back on the bike, and off she goes.

And this is a normally huge, busy street.

Well, she thinks she got away with it, so she did.

But it just adds a laugh to my morning.

Think I'll grab a coffee at a café and do some people watching.

And in the mall you'd watch so many people. Doing some strange things.

How I hate selling seafood.

People like burgers better. Subs too. And Chinese.

Even those Koreans, selling the worst tacos in the world, have a better business going.

I hate the feeling of watching other people have line-ups, and you stand there like a goat.

You get to rationalize a lot.

"They must be putting dope in the food."

Yes, that's it. I'll put $5.00 worth of dope in a $1.00 taco. You'd have to.

Or the staff must be "doing special favors" for the customers.

Nothing to do with the food.

And they're at it again.

OK, so they only have 2 customers, but they're the only 2 in the food court.

It's like an unfair monopoly of some kind.

And the second one's huge, a good order never to be sold!

I hate this feeling.

Time to fantasize about everyone in this city buying 1 fish-n-chips from me so I can retire. I contemplate a wacky appeal to the public.

OK, it won't work. Probably. Money wasted on ads. People approaching me to tell me what a cockroach I am.

"Customer Hefty" is coughing. She looks like a big hippo waiting to be fed.

She's coughing away, and now kind of pacing back and forth behind the other customer.

Stop coughing, please.

Oh no!

Her gum just flew out of her mouth!

Miracle of all miracles, it lands on the other customer's arm!

You couldn't do this if you tried!

Like the Drool King, some of these people's feats defy all!

What's she going to do?

Think quick.

If you had a lot of time to think, you may want to look at the ceiling and pretend it fell from the heavens. Look at the other person very innocently.

But we don't have that much time to think.

Well, what would you do?

Take the gum off the other person's arm, apologize profusely, find a receptacle, deposit spent gum, and disappear, pretending you're not even here.

Right. Probably.

Well, you'd be wrong.

She picks the gum off the person's arm. And puts it back in her own mouth!

All in a split second. Yuck.

Her first inclination was to cover her tracks!

Forget about the other person.

Just because their arm hair sent a message to their brain saying that a gooey substance had made contact with their arm, and then turned to see what appears to be a human picking aforementioned substance off their arm and putting the unidentified flying substance into their mouth, so what?

Happens all the time.

To the credit of the other person, they didn't seem to miss a beat or make anything of it.

To her credit, at least she put it in her own mouth!

What can you do, she wasn't finished with that piece of Stride yet!

Oh well, the cougher's luck does run out.

How?

She buys food from me of course.

"Nice recovery."
"What do you mean?"
When people say this they know exactly what you mean.
"Over there."
"I thought no one noticed."
"I did."
She turned beat red. But stuck around for her food. Then inhaled in at a table.

I tried to act like I admired her ingenuity, but of course I was just plain repulsed.

So, remember, someone is always watching you. Count on it.

I try to remember this now, and try to refrain from scratching my bum before I hand things to people!

Don't forget, it's a new world!

.

Fani California

I made a firm decision not to hire too many female employees.
Our space was just too small, and dangerous. And you had to be able to lift, reach and climb!
You are constantly body-checking everybody. It's 362 sq. ft.

But once in awhile you have a brain-fart!
You do exactly the opposite of what you should do.
So I hired Fani.
What a mistake.

I really feel for the upcoming generation.
I came from the pre-Sesame Street era with mom at home, with the snack after school kind-of-thing.
Today's pre-adult deals with single parenting, the internet, birth control attitudes, cell phones, and blackberrys, widespread venereal diseases, and a higher income world that promotes materialism.

That's a big shopping list.
The good ones are better than my generation.

The bad ones are worse. Way worse. Because of the volume of filth hurled their way, and among other things, the lack of supervision, they are true deviants.

And they make so many bad choices that they effectively ruin their lives just at the point where it really begins.

From an employer's standpoint, this 19 year old was useless—late all the time, weird stuff written on her arms, would only take the customer's money and not do the other 90% of the sale, and so on, ad nauseum.

But she was a nice looking girl, and was fun to have around.

In my day, we collected stamps and played ball.

Today the hobbies are more "interesting."

Fani had certainly developed some intriguing fields of human endeavour.

One of them was explained to me one day by one of my employees, her friend who got her this job!

Fani and a friend have a little hobby/bet going: Who can sleep with the most men?

I'm serious.

At their age the count was 40's for one and in the 60's for the other. Anything goes! And you gradually piece it together. She doesn't know that you know all this, and when her unwanted creepy friends show up at your store, and she acts in a certain way, you can learn to count, too! (Don't need "The Count.")

Another employee informs me she has some incurable form of herpes! I can't imagine how many people she's spread this to!

But she was really "acting out" the role, and one day she informed me she wanted to become a porn star!

I joked that I'd write a script for her, and before we knew it we had pen on paper.

Beyond hokey clichés, our script was bare. It did give us a few laughs, though.

And Fani had an interesting "offshoot" to her hobby.

Fani's mom worked for the city police, a pillar of the community! Hardly.

She and Fani had a simple, yet fun mom-daughter Bonding Activity.
It's simple—The first one who leaves the bar with a man wins!
I'm not sure what the score was there. I wouldn't want to know.
But she gets to notch one up on her other tally, too!
So here's living proof that all that straight and narrow sex talk has something to be said for it. Fani admitted to someone that she couldn't remember half the guys!
And probably for good reason.
These party girls always get their dope for free. It's part of the deal.
And this type of girl soon develops a habit.
Worse still, I suppose, she's always doing different kinds of drugs. More chances for addictions. Who knows what half of it is, anyway?
At least she keeps the drug part of it down while she works for me.

And I come up with an inventive way of getting rid of her!
Fani's family was going on a car trip to a nearby state for an indefinite period.

She wasn't on the store schedule, and we agreed she'd phone later from there or when she got home.
Good.
Just don't put her on the schedule, fill her shifts with someone else, and when she phones tell her we don't need her anymore!
And that's what I did.
I think she was only too happy to be rid of work!

We'd see Fani from time to time. She'd show up with her druggy bum loser friends with heavy cases of the munchies!
You could tell she'd been on some long binge and she was clearly going downhill.
The last time I saw her I was frightened! That's the only word I can come up with.
Fani had now graduated to crystal meth or something on that level.
She'd aged 30 years!
It was bizarre.

And to complement this new look, she had her hair dyed blue-gray! It was something else. She claimed she managed a hotel.

From this to that.

I couldn't believe it.

As the song goes, "Day is gonna come when I'm a gonna mourn ya."

Poor Choices.

Poor Fani.

Fani California.

A Christmas Carol

It was at this time of year that I wished I was a teacher! Or something. Some employ that didn't involve working at Xmas. Imagine all that time off!
November is busy. December is chaos.
At 362 sq. ft., Billy's was a nuthouse! Fries stacked to the ceiling. It was like working on the space station. Two deep fryers, 250-300 customers a day. Madness!
It's not a case of people having their 15 minutes of fame. It's their 15 minutes of shame! It's the mall at Xmas!
If you're going to see people at their worst, it's some episode at the mall in December.
And when they're hungry. And overloaded. And with any number of irritating children, husbands and wives.

And the parking lot is madness.
The mall itself guarantees it.
Every November, they send around a map and regulations telling mall staff where they can and can't park. They even have some kind of contest where obedient staff are in a draw for a prize. The notice comes 4 times or so.

Then they hire part-time "traffic cops" who have no idea what to do!

The last Christmas I was there, they hired staff from a warm country. They put the traffic barriers up for one whole day! It was too cold for them. I saw them shivering and shaking, and running into the building at every opportunity.

One day!

Never heard from again.

And as every seasonal worker in the city probably already had a job, the traffic barriers were never seen again either.

I only laughed at this, as the management of the mall was so inept anyway.

Nevertheless, I still owed myself a break every day. If you were there 14 hours straight, you'd take a break or two.

If it takes 1 hour to enter or exit the mall parking lot, you'd opt for a walk, usually to the beer store.

I must admit our beer consumption sky-rocketed at Christmas! It was easy to only have time to eat once every two days, so the suds kept us going. We figured it was in tune with the spirit of the season. Some of the people we breathed on didn't think so! And we were experts at masking it all. Put someone else on the cash register and Lyle and I would get rocked.

Two months of this cycle.

It was upon return from one of my daily walks that Lyle intercepted me inside the back door and said, "You won't believe it. I told her we don't have any plugs."

Try me. I'd believe anything.

So let's see what I'm going to believe this time.

I walk out to the front counter. It's Dorothy. Good old Dorothy.

In the cartoons, witches come in 2 varieties.

One is the skinny version with the tall, pointy hat.

The other is the plump witch with the fat bulb nose and baggy eyes. She usually likes to boil children and eat them.

Dorothy looks like the latter. And she even wears these funky felt hats that make it look worse.

Like so many others I knew, Dorothy was slowly melting down. Later sometime, she'd tell me she was going to have the Governor make trouble for the mall because someone wouldn't let her borrow (steal) a shopping cart somewhere! The downward slide.

And Dorothy has a present for us. It's a small Xmas tree.

And what looks to be a few cups of tartar sauce! And some napkin cut-outs of our logo!

How thoughtful!

I vaguely remember her asking for a bunch of napkins way back when for some project.

"Ya got no plugs, so I couldn't plug in."

She has a soldering iron in her hand!

A small Xmas tree, tissue paper logos and a soldering iron!

The fact that we have no plugs in the vicinity amazes her. She thinks we are the dumbest people in the world!

Forget the fact that there are 10 machines right in front of her all running on Edison's Dream!

Lyle looks at me.

I look at him.

We are actually quite busy right now, but McGyver is intent on assembling the tree.

Tartar sauce is her new adhesive and she's making a mess out of our counter. Adhering tartar sauce to these finicky little logos and making them stay on needle branches looks impossible! They all slide down the tree and onto the counter.

Dorothy continues to curse us out for not having plugs.

Actually, it would have been better with the soldering iron. We would had the first tree with disappearing ornaments! A little puff of smoke for each one.

It would have been even more amusing explaining it all to the insurance company as Dorothy and her iron gut the place in a fire!

And now Dorothy is drawing a little crowd.

It is rather nice, so I try to appear like this is everyday stuff. I know her well and she's not crazy, kind of thing.

But her 5 or 6 fans are laughing at her, not with her.

And she's not getting it.

THE MALL RAT

And she's enjoying it so much that she gives her phone number to a guy about 20 years old!

Now the peanut gallery is laughing at him. See what you get!

I defuse the situation, change the conversation, and get rid of the spectators to save her dignity—and his.

Dorothy's thrilled as I give her some free food to take home, and display her tree on our cooler, for all to see. For about two minutes.

She's proud she overcome our lack of electricity. She wanted to give us a tree. And she did all right. A glimmer of the true spirit, so to speak. Merry Christmas Dorothy! Merry Christmas to ALL!

A Christmas Peril

'Tis Christmas in the mall.
The heart-warming sight of goods and services being exchanged for cold hard. All those lights and bells ringing...all emanating from cash registers throughout the land.
Six weeks, no it's 7 or 8 now, of mall "Christmas Spirit."
Thank God for Dickens and the Victorians. Who else could supply all the commercial themes these greedy retailers need to push their "made by a poor Non-Christian Kid Somewhere Else" wares?

The history of Christmas is quite fascinating.
Whenever I think about any subject, the first thing I do is think about how long that entity has been around.
Then I picture our view of it, and instantly form a time-line graph of it. With Dickens et al in the mix, we own 10% of Christmas. With the Coca-Cola Santa Era, we are down to 100 out of 2000 years. Five measly percent!
Our version of "Christmas" is quite different from what has been celebrated over the millennia.

And a commercial place needs this.
"Give like Santa and save like Scrooge."

"No payments for 5 years. Ebenezer says."
But I must say it does add a spirit of festiveness to the place.
You yourself are so busy, it's hard to notice what's going on half the time.
And the mall does its best to promote sales.
They're counting on the stores to do a lot of decorating. They do some external stuff, and supply the Secret Service-trained parking lot police.

It's nice to see some of the same faces year after year. The Salvation Army volunteers are always the same couple.
We usually give these types free drinks, free food to some of the more compelling ones.
They all came by a few times over the season for a chat.
Some how we adopted a bugler named Don.
A career bugler. The Boogie Woogie Bugle Geezer.
Every year he'd come around, in dress uniform, and play throughout the mall.
He was quite a character. He loved to play that bugle.
He'd even come to our stall and serenade our customers!
Nice guy.
He even had a CD of his music.
Somehow he even played at Lord Mountbatten's funeral!
So these types contributed to the yearly scene.
The mall hired some entertainment, but they were usually annoying.
Like their carollers.
A threesome, a trio.
They were the loudest, most serious carollers in the history of Christmas. We'd run on sight, they'd actually frighten people. Their singing would actually drown out your conversations with customers!

I like the department stores who have characters greeting you at the door.
Look at him. Worst Scrooge ever.
Mrs. Claus looks like something the cat dragged in.
Or the Santa with shit in his beard.
I watched the Santa in our mall once.
He hated the kids. His nerves were frayed. It was like each kid had Leprosy. Mrs. Claus did most of the work.

We once got a schoolmate of ours fired from such a job.
Good old Wes.
Popular kid in school. Good athlete.
Then he found the weed and acid.
And now he was dressed as Tiny Tim shaking a bell in front of this department store.
And he was a very funny Tiny Tim.
The "I'm a stoner, but I'm trying to be serious" version.
We immediately burst into laughter and went over to him.
The fact that he didn't make much sense, even though he was trying to, made it even funnier.
But he didn't really share in our humor and he was now exhibiting "Piss off and leave" vibes and motions.
No. No. We wouldn't have it.
Let's chat, Tiny Tim!
And all of a sudden this middle-aged man shows up.
"I've been watching you. You're not working. You're fired. Go and take this off and leave."
"But…"
Wes looks at us. Helplessly.
"Time to go. Nice see'in ya again, Wes."
Zoom. Zoom.
We think this is so funny.
I don't think I've ever seen him since.

So it's another busy day in our mall.
You just try to keep everyone happy, get to the end. And regroup.
Today there are some carollers in the courtyard. Kids.
The acoustics in this mall are terrible. For some reason, there is a lot of distortion at ceiling level and it ends at our place.
It sounds like an elementary school group. Young kids, 8 or 9 years old. I see a few of them milling around. Come on the school bus, get organized, and hopefully Grandpa and Granny drive over to the mall to see the kids perform.
It's a pretty harmless Christmas scene. Kind of a pleasant way to pass away the morning.

THE MALL RAT

December mornings are kind of crisp, so the sounds of upbeat music warms you up somehow.

Also puts the shoppers in a better frame of mind. Those sweet little voices tame them a bit.

It's pretty early in the day. Maybe 10:30.
Not much traffic in the food court.
Caregivers like to bring their disabled charges to malls.
It's only natural.
It's indoors. Warm. Stuff to entertain. Services and help, if necessary.
A lot of these people would be regulars in the mall. You'd come to know them.
Lyle liked the guy who always had to "re-boot," as Lyle termed it.
This guy would walk along, and then all of a sudden stop, go dormant, cease.
This would go on for 10-20 seconds, then he'd "re-boot," and resume what he was doing before.
And he'd do this almost at the same place every time! His caregiver would be sitting at a table in the food court.

And it's the same kind of thing today.
A fairly tall stocky black guy, about 20, obviously mentally delayed, is being escorted by a white girl, about 23 or 24.
You can tell by his unresponsiveness that he's pretty slow. Physically, he's all right, he's just moving in slow motion, and can't register much of what's going on.
Poor guy.
I have a lot of empathy for caregivers as well. Doin' the Lord's Work.
Except someone between Social Services and this moment has made a mistake.
A big mistake. It's big all right.
I find it a good idea to play something completely out in your mind before you go do it. Saves you a lot of trouble.
And whoever planned this day didn't take into account that this guy would eventually have to go to the bathroom.
But his caretaker is female.

He's not going to the Women's, she ain't going to the Men's.
I'm not sure if she or they are aware of the Family washroom.
At this point I hardly care.
Or notice them really.
They're just a normal familiar sight.
My mind has only a few basic thoughts, and moves on.
He walks into the washroom area, and she sits on a stool across from Billy's.
And now it's break time for our young choir. No more music.
I see a few of them get off the escalator and walk toward me.
They're going to the washrooms on their break. They look very smart in their uniforms.
It's a clear sunny winter day, and the sunlight is beaming through the skylights.
They're happy and buoyant, glad not to be in school this morning.
I hope they wash their hands, just like mama taught them.

And at this moment you know the world is somewhat screwed!
If anything can go wrong, it will.
You can try to protect your children, but you sometimes can't.
The Theory of Unintended Consequences, the mathematical small chance.
The children going innocently to the bathroom are now going to meet "Chester the Molester," previously known as the slow black guy.

All of a sudden, I hear commotion coming from the side area.
The boys are coming out of the bathroom. Panicking.
Something really bad has happened!
They're looking for an authority figure. A teacher soon turns up.
The group turns back to the washrooms and more boys are coming out.
I can't imagine what these kids have done.
Turns out there's a bad man in the washroom doing bad things!
The caregiver's ears are perking up.
Everyone's heading toward the bathroom area.
Security is being called.
Something really bad is happening.

And out walks Chester.

Doesn't have a clue what's going on.

He merely went into the bathroom, took out his member, and started playing with the boys! Coming up behind them at the urinals. And so on.

This scene is getting ugly.

The boys are freaking out.

The teacher is trying to sort it out.

The caregiver is questioning an oblivious Chester.

Security is now arriving.

And behind all this an old man is shuffling out.

How Hanna-Barbara get it completely right is beyond my comprehension!

He's beet red. No real beads of sweat, but his face is so red you can imagine them. His jaw has dropped. He's speechless and stunned.

And his arms are in front of his face, hands forward, index fingers extended, oh, let me see, about 10-12 inches apart.

I guess when he was a young man they didn't show pornos at stag parties!

He's never seen anything like Chester before!

And he's in shock!

And he's just in the background, somehow adding a very comical touch to this otherwise unfortunate situation.

(Lyle does a very funny imitation of this old guy.)

But it's not that funny right now.

Who's to blame?

In the end Chester walks.

He couldn't care less anyway.

He's been leaning on the Taco counter waiting for these people to move on.

He's bored.

This little conference goes on for another few minutes.

I don't know if they settled anything or not.

They're mostly digging in on their points of view.

Luckily, this is mid-morning and not lunchtime, or they'd have all kinds of people in on the act.

Now it's time to disperse.

The traumatized kids are leaving.

The security guard is still writing down things.

The caregiver is scolding Chester.

The old guy is still in shock. He's even given us a little report in the interim. His shattered innocence continues to be comical!

But now it's over and another mall incident ends.

This mishap was really brought to you by the folks at Social Services. Sending out a female worker with a male patient was just plain dumb.

I wonder if there were any repercussions from this.

I'd freak if my kid came home from school with stories of Chester!

"How was your day at the mall?"

"It was good until we went to the bathroom. Chester rubbed his big thing on little Johnny's bum."

I'd go berserk.

I'd be tracking down the teacher in about 3 seconds!

I wonder where the old man went. Never saw him again. It would be comical to be the fly on the wall listening to him recant his tale to people he meets! He really was priceless.

But it just goes to show, anything can go wrong at any given moment. The piano can land on you, you could meet a swarm of killer bees.

Or go to a mall to sing songs of joy and brotherly love.

That's life.

And in this Corner...

Yeah, Christmas is pretty hectic.

With all the Dorothys and Chesters running around, there's a real carnival atmosphere!

Lots of action. Lots of noise.

Tons of people with tattered nerves! Many of them ask how I can stand the noise. I actually don't mind it. Only the sound of this telephone rattles me! It's never anything good. I especially dislike telephone surveys.

Telephone surveys.

"Can I have a few minutes of your time?"

Exactly.

I can't be giving away my most precious commodity to some stranger at a call center in Bulgaria somewhere.

Once I changed my accent three or four times in one conversation. We could hardly contain ourselves!

Or tell them that Elvis or Jim Morrison is living in your basement. That's a conversation "ender" I use all the time.

I once saw someone scream into the phone. That was fun.

Or simply hang up while you're talking. No one hangs up on themselves.

When it's not hustling and bustling, it feels dead.
And today's another one.
Lots of whiney kids. Red seniors. Seniors hate noise. Little groups of this and that.
The parking lot is chaos. Our mall cops are useless. If you stand and watch them direct traffic, it's quite entertaining.
They get their mickey-mouse hand signals screwed up, which results in either no one moving or everyone moving!
Some smart people don't bother paying any attention to these guys, and barely miss hitting them on the way through!
I usually suck on a couple of brews on my walking-breaks, so these are my clowns.

And the food court is always hot.
And these people are dehydrated.
And they're hungry.
And grouchy.
And on edge.

A woman walks up.
A real nasty one.
She's about 6'2" and sort of "in-my-face." Domineering is the word.
Ok, relax. Your snout will soon be in the trough, Miss Piggy.
Stop glaring.
And here comes another happy customer.
It's National Tall People Day.
This guy's 6'4" or 6'5."
Tall people, sometimes, just cower over you and browbeat you.
Mr. Pushy here is one of them.
Relax.
You'll get fed, park over there by the counter next to Miss Piggy, and soon your dinner will arrive!
He's kind of an ADD type, so he's fidgeting and pacing.
Now he's reaching in front of Miss Piggy and digging into the condiment tray.
I'm right there.

THE MALL RAT

I can see her displeasure.
Granted, it is impolite to reach in front of someone.
But not a huge infraction.
Especially at this time of year.
"You're very rude!"
"What?"
After a few brief verbal jabs, this escalates quickly.
Earl Weaver and Billy Martin.
The saliva's flying!
And then the man kind of "chest-taps" her!
Oh oh.
Technically, he's just hit a woman.
She storms off.
Unbeknownst to us, she's with a man!
A big man.
This dude's 6'8," 245lbs.
Well, at least we don't have to worry about the outcome!
In a flash, he's over to the counter and the chest-tapper is on his ass! A huge push!
No questions asked.
A couple of spits of venom as he approached, but that was it for a warning.
One huge push.
Bye bye.

Now Mr. Idiot's on the floor, appealing to the small crowd that's gathered.
A passer-by disses off his plea.
"Did you see that?," he keeps saying.
"He assaulted me."
He's up now, but he doesn't know what to do.
I'm trying to defuse Mr. Pushy.
"Ok, enough's enough."
But he's ready to punch this guy's lights out.
And he could, too.
Mr. On-His-Bum knows he's going to lose Big Time. But his masculinity has been challenged.

Oh well, you shouldn't have messed with the woman. You big idiot.

So I appeal to him to take the high road and desist. Besides, he doesn't want to go to court with "This Guy" kind of thing.

It works.

It's his way out. (Actually I'd like to see him get his face punched in. He'll only go on disrespecting people.)

There's still a little cussing going on, but they're backing off.

Whew, it's over.

All of that, start to finish, took no time.

One thing led to the next.

The Battle of the Big People.

With little old me in the middle of it, just trying to make a buck.

And now they're backing away making obscene hand gestures at each other.

I love the audience!

They're disappointed their little show is over. Time to go home.

At least no one got hurt.

And the good thing is that they can all disappear, never come back, go on with their day, and enjoy this season of Peace and Love.

That's what Christmas is all about! Reflecting on our fellow humans, and living a life of goodwill and kind gestures.

Like a good hard push and a sincere middle finger!

Ah, that's the spirit.

Hitler Youth

As time goes on, one of my enduring lessons learned at Billy's is the value of having Sundays off!

Every Sunday when I wake up, I'm happy.

When I go out to start the car, it's always sunny.

I'm looking forward to a day of mindless nothing. NFL and pizza sound good.

I appreciate every one of them.

Why?

Because I hated working on Sundays.

I just hated it.

Those of you who work at "unnatural" times know what I'm talking about. But no matter how much you hate working on Sundays, I can assure I loathe it more!

When I first took over Billy's it was very slow. And Sundays were slower. Something like $300 days. My bowels would barely make it home!

And it was the spring of the year and getting warmer. With over 100 machines running in the food stalls, the atmosphere is stifling sometimes.

Standing in an oven making no bread!

I think, even at the end, Sunday was barely a break-even day. Not worth being open unless you have other work to do. Fill in the time.

And I did 5 years worth, less a few. Probably 250 Sundays.

And don't forget you'd always have your worst cooks on.

It's hard to keep your good staff, so it's better not to have them work on Sundays. Lyle would only do it to help me out.

Some of the most laughable food ever went out on Sundays.

Reg's white fries, cooked all of one minute.

I had a few who couldn't cook a single piece of fish without breaking it!

Some of the plates were so mangled, I just couldn't believe it.

Surprise!

"Here's your meal. Enjoy."

How fast can you say that?

And I can't forget the salmon burger going out without the patty. Had to be a Sunday.

It was open-faced. I didn't even ask the "cook" about it until it left.

And the kicker is that the customer didn't even come back to get the "patty"!

They must have thought that the humungous piece of tomato was salmon!

They were foreigners, so I'm sure their conversation must have been very amusing.

In any event, they weren't missing out on much. Salmon is only like the seventh ingredient in the patty. I'm surprised there wasn't a skull and crossbones on the box!

Ah, Sundays.

I really hated them!

And of course Sundays had more than their share of customer missteps.

If Fridays belong to stalkers, Sundays belong to "weirdos."

When I think back over all the weirdos, Sunday would blip on the graph. Big time.

So it's all of the above.

It's a warm Sunday.

I'm working with some half-wit.

And we're not busy.

THE MALL RAT

Just get to 5 o'clock.
And here come the weirdos.

Two ladies come up.
Kind of severe-looking.
One's in her 90's and is barely conscious. Her eyes keep rolling back into her head.
As they "converse," it appears woman number 2 is the daughter.
Yes, I can see the resemblance now.
If you carbon-date one, you may get the other!
And they're speaking in heavily- accented German.
When I grew up, Germans were always the bad guys.
Now, there are hardly any German bad guy movies.
Bring back those German bad guys!
Sadly, the last few alive are sitting in diapers in the Brazilian jungle, singing patriotic songs from their youth.
So I imagine these 2 to be guards at the ladies' prison.
German certainly is abrasive. Looks like it takes a lot of energy.

So now they want to order.
And tell me their story.
It turns out that these two eat at another Billy's. Wowee.
And they love the fish and shrimp.
Great.
Our location actually makes the best looking fish and shrimp.
You think I'm lying, but it's true.
So I suggest this to them.
No. No.
Today, they just want a fish and chips.
I give them all the info on sizes and portions, and they decide to get a 2-piece fish and chips.
I take it by this point in the sale that Granny is none too with it. Must be Alzheirner's or Dementia. And she's fading in and out. She can't remember a thing, and I can tell at one point that she doesn't know where she is.
I always like to guide these sales along, so I tell them how long it will be, where to wait, and so on.

And they shuffle off to the side, talking away in that abrasive accent.

I go about my business.
When I return, I see Granny.
But where's Helga, the she-wolf of Bergen-Belsen?
You've got to be joking.
This woman can't be unattended for more than 10 seconds!
After that, her head is swivelling, and she's mumbling. Well, at least her lips are moving. I think. I hope.
The thought had already crossed my mind that she may not be around to enjoy this food!
Anyway, where's the daughter?
This is insane.
I don't have the time to play attendant.
I don't even know what's wrong with her.
And I'm having a bumming day. She's only the latest in a series of surprises.
I sell food. That's about it. The rest is up to you.
I'm starting to really wonder about the daughter.
Is this some kind of "Nazi Euthanasia"?
Bring Eva Braun to the mall and ditch her!
She's heating up.
It's like she's heavily sedated.

Now, it's time to present the food and say goodbye.
It's now 6 minutes later.
"Control to the Red Baron, where are you?"
And she's about to explode.
Apparently, she thinks she ordered fish and shrimp.
She didn't order anything. "MIA Helga" did.
And speaking of Helga, said Groucho, "Where the hell is Helga?"
Hell if I know.

And Granny is going nuts.
In German.
She's one evil old Granny!

THE MALL RAT

She thinks I can understand German because I have blue eyes and light skin!

Of course I can't understand a word.

And she's semi-preaching to bystanders, who don't know anything about what this woman is talking about.

And she's so demonstrative.

And distorted.

An old monster!

She reminds me of the old Jewish lady chasing Zell in the Gold District in Marathon Man. In reverse.

That voice.

That shrill voice.

Except this old thing doesn't get clobbered by a vehicle. I never experience Olivier's relief!

We're now past 10 minutes.

Granny's having a flashback to the Nuremberg Rallies.

She's quite animated.

Where's the (expletive) daughter?

Hopefully, only gone shopping.

I "appeal" to passing members of the general public, who look at me like it's the last thing they'd ever do.

And the more I don't understand, the more riled up she gets.

And, it's one of these Mexican standoffs where she keeps insulting the food in German, and I keep offering it to her. In the same dumb way.

Oh, she's back.

It's only been 20 minutes.

Granny's had a pretty busy time. Made lots of new friends.

I'm worn out.

Auf Wiederzehn.

No way.

It's time for Round 2.

One in German, one in English.

Now it's time for the fish and shrimp argument.

This goes nowhere.

Going off, they take the food and leave.
Thankfully.
It's Sunday. I don't need this.
If you're taking Granny to the mall, at least remember what's she eating. Oh yes, new shoes. And some make-up. Hey, it's a sale.
Anyway, they're angry.
I just hope she's so busy with Granny tomorrow that she doesn't have time to complain.

No such luck.
The full force of Stalag 13 comes down to me!

And it comes in the form of, who else, the Marketing Lady.
This is so painful.
Apparently, Florence Nightingale took Mother Theresa to the mall to eat at your restaurant. They always eat there! At which time I was the meanest person ever to this sweet old senior.

I can't win.
The Marketing Lady must be smiling like a Cheshire Cat.
And the fish Nazis hit Billy's Head Office up, too!
And no matter what you say in your own defence, you are screwed.
Little Old Ladies are one of the "Holy Grails."
My own stupidity sickens me. This is a PR disaster.
I especially like how the Marketing Lady recants some of the more memorable lines to me. "I will never shop at this mall again." The ML loves it!

How much money did I make on Sundays?
Negative something.
And look at this shit!
You simply can't predict 60,000 sales a year.
But the damage is done.
The Bad Guys win.
I don't want to see any more German bad guy movies.
Remember this one.

The Handyman

Who can screw the Church up?
(Who can screw the Church up?)
Kill everything in bloom?
Kill everything in bloom?
Who can turn your day into misery and gloom?
The Handyman can.
Yes, the Handyman can.
The Handyman can.

Why did I do this?
The Yellow Pages are there for a reason.
And that reason is to find reputable goods and services when you need them.
I didn't do this.
I saw little ads on pieces of cardboard fastened on little wooden stakes. On the side of the road.
For a "handyman." With a phone number.
And our taps are broken again.
On. Off. On. Off. All day long.

Two or three times a year they'll go.
This gets expensive.
So I think I'll give this "handyman" a try.
He's probably an old retired guy who can do anything. And he's probably not up on modern pricing, so I'll get a bargain.
Oh yeah.
I'll offer him some food to get the price down. Maybe he's just happy to have something to do and he won't even charge me!

So I phone the number.
The guy says he knows all about plumbing and he'll be over.
Year 8 of the 10-Year "Crack Montage" turns up.
My previously hard, evil Gothic employees are now shaking sissies!
I must admit he is pretty scary.
"Intervention" wouldn't have him.
Neither would "Sober House."
An addict only a mother could love!

But I'll give him a chance. Help the downtrodden and all that.
He says he has to get parts.
He goes.
He comes back.
He takes everything apart.
Puts it back together.
No dice.
The taps don't work.
Don't worry, he'll get the right part and fix it tomorrow.
He comes back a few days later.
Still no dice.
But he's determined.

I'm starting to doubt his ability to do this job, and I tell him he may want to forget about it. I'll give him a few bucks and so on.
He won't hear of it.
He now wants to take the taps to his "workshop" or whatever.
At least he won't be here scaring people!

THE MALL RAT

I have no faith in him, but I figure he'll just give up at some point.
The crack and the booze have corroded his mind.
I haven't heard from him in a few days. Probably on a bender.

And then one day there's a knock on our door.

I answer.
No one there.
I look down.
What do I see?
Like a cartoon orphan lies the taps!
In a few pieces!
Do I hear "Lullaby"?
He's gone.

No explanation needed. He's the handyman.

Bono

A man's gotta know his limits.
No truer words have ever been spoken by Clint.
The person who realizes the limitations of the situation is far ahead.
You can even go high, one step at a time.
But a man's gotta know his limits.
And sometimes you see glaring examples of things like this. Bad examples.
In things such as knowing the limits.
And this comes in the form of a stalker.

In a lifetime you can play infinite roles, but I know "Bono" as a stalker.
He's "Bono" because he wears yellow and orange wraparounds. Indoors. If that bothers you. Doesn't bother me. Makes you easy to spot.
Besides that, he's a loner in his early fifties who reads a bit. Old looking, ruddy complexion.
I don't know when Bono first came around.
It seemed like he was there forever.
He was like clockwork. Like no other person I observed in the mall. It was the focal point of his day.

THE MALL RAT

When he woke up, he looked forward to this great event.
After he left, he was aglow.
Whatever was going on in the rest of the day was not all that important.
Bono could have been a good guy. I don't think I ever talked to him.
I saw Ayn Rand in his hand one day. So he must be reasonably intelligent.
But you have to know the limitations.
And Bono didn't.

If Bono went to the library sometimes, he might have met a girl named "Agnes," who works there part-time. And so on . Met someone suitable.
Blah, blah.
Not Bono.
He gets himself in the worst possible mental situation: He becomes fixated on a girl that will be impossible to land.
Impossible!
And he's fixated.

And the object of his desire works at a coffee shop.
And sometimes you see elements of just plain bad luck.
For I've noticed that coffee is something you can buy every single day. Or more often than that even.
So the stalker has a real bonus card here.
He'd be attracted to her anyway, this just makes things easier.
"I just love coffee."
Yes sirree.
So that's about all I know about Bono.
But I do know something about his heart's desire.
She's 35 years younger, and Asian.
Without being mean, or anything, I really can't see these 2 together at the altar.
Whatever is going through Bono's mind is just plain off base.
Now, for the betting public, I'll whisper some inside information in your ear!
Besides having virtually nothing in common, there's one little fact that will trump the hand.
She comes from a family of Arranged Marriages.

This girl will be marrying someone else.
I'm pretty sure of that.
I'm also pretty sure Bono doesn't know this.
Strangely, I know this about the girl before I really even meet her.
And I never ask her about it.
Not my business.
If she wanted me to know, she'd tell me.

I got coffee there many mornings over the 2 years she was there, and I talked to her many times, but I never asked her personal questions.

So I'm watching a real mismatch.
And as I said, I can't even remember when Bono started coming around.
And it was the same routine. Over and over. And over.
I'm at the apex of a V. The coffee shop is halfway up the right side.
Bono enters top left.
The interior of the V is filled with raised seating.
Visually obscured, you'd have to be looking for something or someone in particular to look in that direction.
So she never sees him coming everyday.
She's doing whatever.
He comes in from the top left.
He even has a little spark in his stride.
Sometimes more than that, and he bounces along.
Not that he cares, but even the bouncing along will make people notice you.
If I had a nickel for every time Lyle and I would identify a customer by way of some small attribute!
An expression, a tick, any mannerism.
I once identified a man to another mall worker in the following way:
"He's a big Goof."
It worked.
It was actually the right guy.
This fella drove a Disabled Bus so he could sell Avon products to his captive audience!
He told me he was the No. 1 Avon man in the State.
Buddy, you're the only Avon man in the state!
He quickly became the "Avon Laddie."

THE MALL RAT

A real "Goof."
I digress.

Bono is oblivious. It's just him and his love interest.
What a train wreck!
It's always the same.
Enter stage left, bouncing along.
As soon as he enters the food court, his head darts hard left.
Is she here?
She is.
He smiles away, and walks toward me.
It's just after 2:00, no need to look at the clock!
And he walks past, and goes to the washrooms.
Four to five minutes, every time.
He emerges from the washrooms and does a "thinking walk" over to the coffee chop.
Bono's really in a fantasy world.
And he always begins the trek from my counter to the coffee shop with this glazed look on his face. I'm next to the washrooms, so his journey begins right here.
I don't know whether this is the result of a prescription he's taking, or what. H e's trippin'.
His noggin is 6—8 feet away from me, every day. I get to see this look all the time.
It would have been interesting to take a picture every day, and then run them in sequence in a movie. In 20 seconds.

And he's off!
He gives himself a wide berth over everyone, but he's still prone to bumping into people.
I wonder what he's thinking about…
Aah…he's reading Marshall McLuhan by the fire. She's serving coffee or tea, and his favorite gingersnaps.
As she's "serving him," you have to imagine The REAL look on her face! Fright. Wake up.
And coffee can be purchased every day.

You have to look at it from her point of view.

Every day, at a certain time, this creepy dude who makes you very uncomfortable shows up.

Every day.

And you have to serve him.

And talk to him.

And if there's no one around, he'll linger and make small talk.

Sometimes he'll plant himself for an hour and read.

I once gave an employee the following advice: Cut your losses. Get out. Every time you're around that girl, she recoils and moves back. She's afraid of you (for good reason).

I would have given Bono the same advice.

There's no hope.

You will marry this girl in circumstances not to be found. Alone on a desert island, an impossibly rich Bono who's terminally ill. She'd blindfold the monkeys even. "Sign this."

Why am I always the "Designated Observer"? Why do I have this stupid surreal position where I just happen to be around enough for all of the episodes to put it all together.

And the time goes on.

And one day I'm getting my morning coffee.

And the girl at the counter tells me she's leaving soon to get married to someone overseas.

No surprise to me.

She asks me if I think it's possible to fall in love with someone you've never met.

I answer "maybe."

My split second logic thinks anything is possible, stranger things have happened, and with the divorce rate, it's worth a shot.

So my bad luck holds out long enough to witness her telling him she's leaving. It's a sad day.

The coffee shop is 60 feet away. My vantage point, with the angle, is just a little too good.

Luckily for her, the timing and length of his daily visits is such that she leaves unimpeded.

If she's smart, her ride is waiting at the door.

THE MALL RAT

The times I've seen her talk to Bono outside the perimeter of the coffee shop her hands have been folded in from of her, low in front of her torso. A defensive position.

I think way back in the mists of time he may have tried to approach her on an "outside the coffee shop relationship," but no advance was met with success. Maybe, who knows?

And now his bubble is bursting!

I can tell she's giving him the news.

The way he turns around and leaves is sad.

He's shattered, but trying to put on a brave face.

Why do I have to watch this?

On the other hand, it's his own fault. Your chances of success were zero, and all you did was irritate this girl for ages.

But he still comes around.

His demeanor has changed.

Now he's more excited.

His relief after he spots her is tangible.

He walks faster. No time to waste.

When he emerges from the washrooms, he's more haggard and desperate- looking.

I'm guessing this girl isn't going to miss this.

And the day arrives.

An elderly customer comes to give "Miss Bye-Bye" a cake.

It's her last day.

It's nice when people turn up on your last day to wish you well.

I don't bother, as it looks like she has lots to do on her last day. Usually, it's handing off your duties, getting your pay, and exchanging addresses and numbers with people you never contact again!

And Bono turns up.

She's down to an hour or two. I bet she can't wait to leave. I'd crack open a few cold ones in the car in the parking lot!

To add to the circus, her only other identifiable "love interest" turns up at the same time!

This is "The Twizzler."

A Twizzler is sort of a dork interloper who doesn't know his behaviour is inappropriate.

I don't know how the Twizzler sleeps at night.

I really don't.

If I drank that much coffee I'd never sleep. Ha, ha.

The Twizzler is a white kid in his twenties who looks like Dennis the Menace.

Two thousand cups of coffee later he's joining Bono. In the eleventh hour. True Disciples.

To round out the cast we have the Dirty Old Man who owns the place.

It's quite a sight!

Well, time for me to leave for my afternoon break. I'll just switch my set off, so to speak, and go do something else.

She'll be gone and he'll find new life somewhere else.

It is sad, but Bono should have realized this in the beginning. Obsession clouded the judgement of this man. I can't help ya. If he'd asked me, I would have told him to go find Agnes.

Only he doesn't believe she's gone!

I should have seen this coming, too.

She's now on a plane going to Asia, and he's still here!

She doesn't know that, never will.

The new workers don't know this guy or don't care. His attempts at making conversation and getting information from them are met with indifference.

But I, the unlucky one, get a ring side for the show. Start to finish. And beyond.

Your mind must be total jumble to do this.

Even if she lied to you, don't you think she had a reason?

Nope. He knows she's coming back!

She isn't.

This is painful to watch.

His visits slow to a trickle.

But never quite stop. He just can't let go.

THE MALL RAT

Now it's our last week in the mall. We're leaving. Time to pack up.

It's a stressful week, and Lyle and I are now blowing off steam by watching Clint Eastwood movies and drinking cheap beer after work. I highly recommend it.

And the boy's getting a great Eastwood 101 lesson.

I'm pulling into the Blockbuster parking lot to return one of our rentals. It's 10:00.

There's a book store, a large box one, in the parking lot.

Who's coming out?

Bono. Book in hand.

As I drive to Blockbuster, I notice a group of young people near cars. About 10 of them. They're Asians.

My car is cheap, so I can hear lots of things going on outside the car.

And this group is quite loud.

I drive past, drop off another Clint favorite, and drive on out.

As I near the exit, Bono is getting in his car.

But he isn't.

He's peering at the group of kids by the car.

He's so intense.

It's dark. There's no way you could identify anyone. They all look the same anyway.

But that's what he's doing.

He's trying to see if SHE is one of them!

And he's really obvious, sneaking looks around the top of his car!

Yeesh, he is really creepy!

Well, we are finished in the mall in 2 days, anyway.

I never see Bono again.

So many times I see these start to finish stories, in an in-the-now, surreal way. The fly on the wall. Ongoing. Episodal.

Poor guy. A man's got to know his limitations. Bono still hasn't found what he's looking for.

She lives on, "A street with no name."

Not yours!

Ah, Limitations!

The Garden of Eden

I read the newspapers everyday.
If I'm in a foreign country, I'll read theirs.
The T.V. can only provide so much education.
I speed -read so I can cover it all in a few minutes.
Look for the key words.
What's this in the business section today?
Well, some uber-rich German bank is buying into 10 of our landlord's malls to the tune of half a billion bucks. Big plans to invest and expand!
For a second or two I have this fantasy of Germans in suits on my doorstep with briefcases of money, opening them for my approval!
Oh well, we'll see.
Maybe there'll be something in this for us.
Oh, there will be!
You see, one of the off- spins of the yet-to-be-announced renovation project will be us being pushed off the cliff!
But I digress.
This is only the third year of my occupancy in the mall, so the real writing on the wall hasn't been brought to my attention as of yet.
I mention this news story to a few people at the mall, but evidently they don't read the newspaper.

THE MALL RAT

I have plenty of other things to occupy my mind, so this news tidbit falls to the wayside.

Maybe something happens, maybe nothing happens.

I have a business to run, so I won't think too much about this for the time being.

About the time I've completely forgotten about it, a memo arrives from the mall administration announcing a fabulous $ 135 M Renovation Project. Meeting to follow.

The 135 eventually balloons to 200, with the tenants left holding the bag. Of course. The big news is that the food court is moving!

The landlord is lord of the land. The tenants have no say in how this money is spent. It's divide and conquer. All 200 of you.

I don't bother going to the meeting.

There's usually nothing of importance going on. The people on stage act like they're addressing the U.N. Living off the fat of the land.

And the mall always sends a package around later. Or 2. Or 3. Or 4.

I'm glad to see our mall is partially wind-powered. Signs everywhere telling the public that. Wow.

Most businesses that tell you how green they are are only selectively sampling their business practices. If you looked at the whole operation, you'd see a radically different picture.

And I always get the low-down from the older man who owns the Chinese place. He knows everything.

He reminds me of a Mafia Don.

Unassuming. Down to earth. Only shows up to collect money kind of guy.

And he knows everything.

He's been in food and malls for 35 years.

Interestingly, he was originally an engineer who built the mall we're in! The food business came from his involvement in designing the place.

And he's been in other malls and businesses, so he's a real authority on what's what.

I call him "Confucius."

He's the only business owner in the food court who I actually seek advice from. He always gets it right.

And the Great Sage doesn't like it.

At all.

He prophesizes that we, the tenants, will be left holding the honorable bag!

And the food court operations don't pay much rent.

As a business expense, rent is major for us.

But one good second level store pays as much rent as the whole food court combined!

Why spend millions relocating businesses where the payoff isn't all that large?

It gets worse.

The plan only calls for 2 new stores. For $135 million. Are you nuts?

A mall 3 miles away is spending $280 million. And getting 80 new stores. You do the math.

It's all going to be about "cosmetics." New floors. New this. New that.

Most of those things were replaced a few years ago. They're fine, even to my critical eye.

The outside could stand a little attention.

The brick walls are stained in places because of things like signage. Water stains.

Otherwise, the mall is good. It's clean. It's modern.

The plan should be to add square footage and parking.

But the plan is to just change everything around in the same square footage. A home reno.

This is dumb.

No businessman would do this.

There's no upside.

Nicer floors aren't going to bring in one single customer.

New stores will, though.

But relax, we, the tenants are just too dull-witted to grasp their vision. We are imbeciles.

The package arrives from the mall. It's all Architects' Drawings. The lines hurt my eyes and it eventually collects dust somewhere.

I can't understand any of it anyway.
Where at you putting the bookstore?
Why this? Why that?
I do notice that they are moving Customer Service.
Presently, it is situated near a main entrance.
Now, it's going to be in a back hallway!
Shrewd.
Now those lazy people can kick back without the nuisance of those pesky shoppers!
This is actually one of the few projects that comes to fruition before I leave.
And it's secluded.
And posh.
The chairs. The T.V. screens.
New A/C.
And now businesses situated near the entrances become new little Customer Service Agents!
I'm actually surprised that the people at the top approved all these plans.
It's like giving a huge budget to people who are addicted to home improvement shows.

And all these cosmetic changes are subject to blunders and rip-offs.
Don't like the color?
Hey, we'll repaint it 50 times. And charge you 50 times.
In fact, the more mistakes the better.
The general contractor in this one makes a fortune.
It's carte blanche.
Once they get going, it's like a runaway train!
One of my friends at the mall was a guy who was a sort of permanent tradesman, who had contracts with the mall.
He'd give me all the funny, ridiculous stories of how they would stumble from one screw-up to the next, haemorrhaging money at every corner.
All parties involved could see the chance to fill their pockets. And they did.
Let's install new escalators.
That are the wrong size.

Oopsy.

Let's redo almost every granite tile in the mall.

With the wrong tiles.

Oopsy.

Now it's like a skating rink.

Apparently the supplier screwed-up and supplied the wrong tiles.

This is not a minor mistake!

The finish on the tiles is wrong.

People start slipping and falling.

The injury lawyers descend on the mall, asking clerks in stores to be witnesses!

I'm not making this up.

They try and do something to make the tiles grittier.

To no avail.

And they're not even levelled properly. Millions of dollars later there's tape on the floors to prevent people from tripping.

In some places the tiles will have to come up, and are replaced by carpeting.

And the tenants will be stuck with it all.

Think about the brilliance of it. You go from tiles to tiles to tiles and carpeting!

I notice that in the Artist's Rendering I saw a Starbucks, front and center.

I hope the other coffee venders realize they'll soon be toast.

And they are.

It ends up being a mall with no bookstore. No bookstore!

I can't believe it.

The bookstore has to go to make way for the new super-dooper "pillow shop."

Every thing you could possibly screw up, these folks could.

And the contractors and mall administration people strut around like Roman Emperors. It's comical. The blind leading the blind. Actually, the smart leading the blind.

And they're even going to build a strip mall in one of the parking lots. I bet that'll bring in a lot of customers.

THE MALL RAT

But so will isolating the new Food Court on the second floor of a new wing in another parking lot!

Half the time you didn't know whether to laugh or cry!

I overheard a foreman talking on his cell phone one night as I was leaving.

Evidently, someone had forgotten to rent some piece of equipment.

No problem, he said, in his best union voice.

His crew was merely going to sit down and do nothing all night!

Remember, this work is being done at night. So the minimum wage here is over $30 an hour. Some of these guys get $40 or $50.

More power to them, but a quick calculation says $3000 will vanish overnight. For nothing.

And that's a "nothing cost."

Most of the screw-ups run into the tens and hundreds of thousands.

The money vanishes.

No one looks to be responsible.

There's no reason to be.

The tenants will pay it.

And so it went. A gradual bleeding to death.

And these renos are now done over years.

So a person with a 5-year lease can be involved in this traffic killing exercise for 3 or 4 years. It's insane.

While probably not the most expensive blunder, (the tiles will take it "hands down," literally and figuratively!), the most intriguing project had to be "The Garden of Eden."

Ah, the Garden.

This was a piece of ground between a road and a parking lot.

On a slope.

About 200 long, 40 wide.

With mature trees.

A foot-worn path.

Natural looking, green, the trees holding the soil.

And one day I see a crew.

With tree-removing gear.

Bye bye trees.

This is now going to be some kind of modern rock world. It's going to be developed, one of those miniaturized odes to about 10 different fads.

No more green space or trees, it's cement, huge rocks and rails.

Knowing our mall is 25% wind-powered makes me feel better, though.

And so it begins.

Let's get rid of the bank altogether.

That's a lot of earth.

That's a big mess.

Then the job started.

Someone designed this urban park concept with these Stonehenge rock things. Wow.

And the shrubs are here.

Two trees here.

A concrete walkway with steps and a rail. The rail was added.

It was added after they moved the location of the path.

They moved the path a few times.

And everything else, too.

And the parade of heavy equipment trucks never ends.

For weeks on end.

Huge flatbeds doing all kinds of things, at $300-$500 per hour.

And it would go on forever.

Then the crews would disappear.

But then reappear again.

Time to move the path.

Blast that concrete, rip up those bushes.

And this is all over a nothing piece of land that probably should have been left alone in the first place!

These companies are filling their pockets.

It's in direct view of our smoking area, so we can watch the laughable amounts of "work" being done.

And they could really do some funny things.

The area was installed with a modern irrigation system. These things probably waste lots of water, shady trees provide green grass in our climate. Naturally. Water from above.

But one morning I drive in and the huge adjoining parking lot is totally flooded.

It seems they were testing the system the night before and it malfunctioned!

It also seems that they didn't leave anyone behind to see if it would malfunction!

My memory of this was the poor old shrubs, all washed down the hill, clinging to the curb.

Don't worry, they'll be in the garbage as soon as this flood is under control!

I don't think I mentioned our mall is 25% wind-powered.

Of course the inside of the mall is flooded, too.

Anyway, the companies involved in this venture soldiered on, ranking in the money, no pun intended.

And I just couldn't figure it out.

Just when you thought it was finally over, it would begin anew.

This 8000 sq. ft of land had taken on a life of its own.

And one day I got an answer.

I just couldn't figure out why countless changes were necessary to this piece of land.

What's your guess?

If you get it, you can go to the head of the class.

It turns out our landlord has moved offices to the tower on the property.

It's a pretty cheesy office tower, so they're occupying it themselves. No one else wants to.

And that 8000 sq. ft of land is their view!

I'm serious.

So now we have a bunch of Martha Stewarts on the 8th floor way over yonder doing some urban rock thing!

This is insane.

But it's the only answer. Someone with clout.

The person telling me all this knows someone who works there, and tells me all the ridiculous anecdotes that go along with it.

They've all watched hours of those home improvement shows, and now the experts are building their creation!

Those shows should be banned.

You see gays hammering nails one day.

The next it's midgets.

Then it's limbless people who hammer with their nostrils.

And now all these creative juices are let loose on this innocent plot of land!

But at least I have an answer.

To this one.

The mall has many little projects to amuse and challenge your brain.

And it continues long after we're gone.

I rarely go over to the mall.

I don't shop much.

But I do go the Ticketmaster once in a while.

It's at Customer Service, conveniently located near nothing. But I do like the A/C.

The last time I was there I slipped rounding a corner.

Me!

They even have "Caution—Slippery Floor" signs everywhere.

Me!

I'll wear my skates next time.

And a helmet.

Hey, I smell a good insurance scam here.

Anyway, gotta run.

I mean fall.

It Took Four Years

People in retail have a rough life.
Constantly on the receiving end of some less-than-polite complaint or comment.
And you are always wrong.
One lady brought back a plate that had a shard of fish, two fries, and a 15" black hair laid perfectly across it!
"There's a hair in my food."
There's no source for this hair around here. If I started sprouting 15" long hairs, I'd probably go see a doctor.
And more than once an almost empty plate would be returned with an "It's Too Fishy" complaint!
What the "H" does that mean?
It's a Fish Store.
Guess what we sell?
I especially like when a customer belches, "Wwhherre's mmy rreefiill?"
Brian aptly classifies them as "soulsuckers."
It's your biggest day-to-day challenge as a shop-keeper.
Of course human beings don't always run on logic, or self-interest.
So they complain.

And complain.

You have no inclination to put much into the sale.

I've long since learned that the cheerful customer gets.

It's all very simple.

I'm going to be one of the few happy customers all day. I don't have any problems.

If a store doesn't have it, I go somewhere else. If you're out of it, I'll order something else. If you bring the wrong thing, I'll eat it anyway. Without complaint. I always leave a good tip, and never complain until after I pay the bill. I politely point out the flaw. If I go back, I go back.

And this attitude wins. Whatever freebies or upgrades can be given away, you are going to be one of the recipients. This system generally takes care of itself.

But don't tell anyone. There's only so much stuff to go around!

And you just used to listen to petty, nonsensical hohums from these petty, nonsensical hohums.

How many times will I suffer through the accusatory, "I wanted Diet Coke. This is Coke" line.

And you have to pick up the now empty cup and fill it again with Diet Coke.

And then one day it happened.

A customer finally admitted they were wrong!

I was totally taken aback.

I had listened to so much "scrooge-talk," that what my ears now heard shocked me.

I presented a man's tray of food to him and thanked him for his business.

He was an Oriental man about fifty. "I'll have a Coke for my drink, thank you."

"I'm sorry sir. This meal doesn't come with a drink."

"My mistake. I'll have a medium Coke, please."

And he reaches for his wallet.

I can't believe it.

What's wrong with this guy?

THE MALL RAT

He's supposed to launch into a tirade about how the meal came with a drink "last time," how our advertising is misleading, or that he wants a refund if I don't give him a drink.
Nope.
This guy is going to purchase a beverage to consume with his meal!
I don't know what to do.
I burst into laughter.
I give him the drink for nothing.
He doesn't quite get it.
The Meek do indeed inherit the Earth. Sometimes, anyway.
Someone had finally admitted they were wrong.
It took four years.

Who's Your Daddy

Human sexuality.

The Law of Attraction.

What attracts one person to another is one of those elusive questions, for sure!!!!!

In my opinion, it starts too young and goes on too long.

The young don't know what they're feeling. And the old aren't feeling anything at all.

And "women" develop earlier. And live longer. They're a different breed, that's for sure!

And in a mall business, you just deal with so many people. You get to encounter all the fringy types.

My favourite was this psycho-horny old lady.

She's in her 60's. Tanning salon. Shirt open in an old-lady sort of way.

I don't even dare look at this.

She's been here before.

Last time she was here she hung off to the right side and glared at me, sorry, my eyes, for an eternity.

And she's back.

THE MALL RAT

There's a nice-looking woman in front of her. About 20.
It's a sad world when the one that's interested in you is the booby prize! I must be losing my touch.
Hottie orders and moves over to wait.
Here she comes.
C'mon now, you have to at least blink.
There you go.
This is really uncomfortable.
Why don't you limp down to the home and play bridge.
"And here's your change. You can wait right over here."
This waxy-dummy has been 18-24 inches from my face for a couple of minutes.
She's in a trance.
Maybe she's one of the Manson Grannies.
Anyway, she's not leaving.
It's like I'm in a stare-down with the "Amazing Whoever."
"Anyway, the show's over."
I actually said that!
And I point her to the waiting area.
The Hottie thinks I'm mean.
I think she's hot.
I also think this old lady is in some altered-state.
The Hottie snatches the bag out of my hand and gives me a dirty look.
Ah, I never liked you anyway!
Now, I'm left with this obsessed old lady.
She gawks at me some more, and eventually slithers away.
I think the shamelessness of it caught my attention.
Those old men at the home better be careful.
I guess it all makes sense.
In high school, there are the "easy" girls.
I guess the same goes for seniors' homes.
Some of them probably still frequent lingerie shops. And worse.

Malls always have 2 or 3 lingerie shops.
None of the customers remotely look like the posters on the wall.
It's a "Dream Factory."

The male equivalent is the sporting good store.
I like the really huge women with the little, tiny lingerie bags.
Inside the bag looks to be an even tinier article of cloth with frills on it.
Should I call the U.N.?
"Hello, World Cop. I'm phoning to report A Crime Against HuMANity. It's in progress."
Sometimes I don't know whether to laugh or cry.

But at least with adults you know the score.
At the other end of the spectrum, the little girls are all into it.
Girls develop earlier than boys.
And with the tinkering of our food by the conglomerates, girls are developing even earlier.

A T.V. show informed me that the original Twinkies had 4 ingredients.
Today's version has 42. Something like that.
Twinkies. Meat. Everything.
These little girls have breasts.
And by the time they should be getting breasts they've graduated on to cosmetic procedures and the rest.
And it shows.
These little girls are trying to hustle you like everyone else. The chemicals go to their brains, too.

I served a woman who had a nice silent little girl with her.
"Here's your change. And you can wait over here."
They move to the side, where Mom deposits the daughter on the counter while she plays with her phone.
I don't really like this. It's against the Health Code. Sometimes these sweet children have inadvertently used the bathroom. Just not in the bathroom.
Sometimes you can even smell it.
It kind of lingers in over the counter. Invisible fog.
And if they fall off the counter, who's responsible?
Hopefully not me.
So I hang around that end of the counter.

THE MALL RAT

"You're a boy."
"I am."
"And I'm a girl."
"You are."
"No. You're a boy."
"Well, I am."
"And I'm a girl," she purrs.
Good. Well, we've established 2 facts.
"You're a boy."
"Well, actually, I'm a big boy. I am a man."
"No. You're a boy," she hisses.
"O.K. I'm a boy. But I'm also a man," I say weakly.
"No. You're a boy."
Why am I involved in this? Can Mom get off the phone and rescue me from this 5 or 6 year old terror?
"And I'm a girl," she sings.
You're a nuisance, and I'm fed up is more like it!
"You're a boy."
You're a pain in the derriere.
Finally the food rescues me from absentee Mom, and this little bundle of innocent but disconcerting hormones.

There's some bunch of little boys playing in a tree house somewhere, reading comic books, who have no idea of what is in store for them!

Worse than this was a little girl who kept calling me "Daddy."
Momma Bear hauls up with this 3 year girl.
Places her feet right on the counter and holds her from behind.
"Daddy, Daddy."
I try to ignore her.
"Daddy, Daddy, Daddy."
I look at Mom.
"Daddy, Daddy, Daddy."
Mom thinks it's amusing and smiles.
She only has a few more teeth than the kid, so I think I know where the Daddy crisis is coming from.
And this kid is really loud.

And continues on.
"Daddy, Daddy, Daddy."
She's now lunging at me.
People are looking at us.
They might even think I'm related to these two!
Or this is some kind of paternity deal and "toothless" here is shaming me into the child support payments!
"Stand over here now."
"Daddy, Daaaddy, Daaaadddy."
Shut your hole.
I'm not your Daddy, you out of control robot.
But they don't leave.
And now a man I believe could be the Daddy comes up.
The kid continues.
He thinks it's cute, too!
Now I know you're all nuts!

As usual, the arrival of the food bails me out.
With a full set of teeth between them, they depart.
A woman, a child and a man.
Who's the Daddy?
Not me.

How's the Clam Chowder?

Everyone sells stuff they're not particularly proud of.

It's nice to present an attractive meal, or make a big sale, but sometimes people buy things that you'd sooner not sell!

Hands down, it was the clam chowder for us.

The clam chowder.

When I was growing up, I was always in my father's warehouse.

This was a chinaware importing business, and hay or straw was used as packing material for eons.

That smell will never, ever leave my olfactory memory. That sweet smell of hay.

Or my great-uncle's pipe.

Or that sickly smell of Billy's clam chowder!

Sick was the word. Ill, putrid, nauseating, uncomfortable and nasty also qualify.

There was nothing redeeming about it.

The way it goes is this.

Every fast food chain likes to sell every conceivable item that can be associated with their core product.

And everyone sells chicken.

Chicken fingers, chicken dinosaurs, chicken chickens, chickens who aren't chickens, and so on.

Everyone sells chicken.

And every chain tries to beat their turf to death. It's basically an effort to disguise the core product. Yet again. And again.

I love ads on T.V. where the opening frame is "NEW."

How "NEW" is it really?

It's yesterday's product twisted around by the fingers of some ad hoc "team" in an impromptu kitchen back at Head Office in New York. Authentically Mexican.

And for Billy's the move into soups and chowders was a natural.

But of course no one is actually going to make a soup or a chowder, they're just going to flip open the food company's catalog and pick one out.

Expediency plays a role in a lot of decisions, so Head Office people usually pick items they imagine are easy to prepare, sell, and maintain.

Wrong on the chowder, folks.

It's hard to make, no one wants it, and it doesn't stay "fresh" very long.

Our clam chowder is made by a national food company.

It comes in frozen blocks.

Yummy.

If you're a polar bear.

If you're not, you're holding a frozen block of potatoes.

That's the only admirable thing about it. How a group of "researchers" at the soup company managed to get a bunch of chemicals and a few potatoes to hang out together like this. The miracles of modern science.

The cooking instructions are simple.

Put the frozen block in a pot and add milk.

Cook it in a double boiler kind of operation to a certain temperature, and then maintain it on a hot table.

Sounds simple.

It's a disaster.

Our stove is at the end of the line, so no one ever checks on the chowder.

Especially if we're busy.

It's just screwed up.

You never know what kind of "batch" it's going to be due to the level of negligence involved in making it!

One problem is that water keeps boiling up and spilling into the chowder.

This water is filled with charred pieces of the pot due to the fact that we burn up every pot. We're idiots.

That's pretty much the cycle.

About one month after I bought the place I was alarmed to see something orange in the chowder and called Lyle out. He informed me that the orange thing was a clam!

I'd previously thought the clams were one of the white things in the chowder! I saw one clam in one month.

Lyle loved to recite the complaint this stupid old English guy gave him.

"I have to tell you this because no one else will. You have the worst clam chowder I've ever had. You should call it "Potato Chowder." That's what it really is."

And Lyle loved his own English accent. It's a tour of England. Cockney to Aristocrat.

And no one bought the chowder, so its cycle of disgustingness was pretty much assured.

If we sold three times the product it would have worked.

But it never came to be. Like our "coffee."

And it was expensive in terms of food cost, so we'd never throw it out. Sorry.

It was quite common to have three different "vintages" mixed together.

Separated, lumpy, and mystery lots were constantly mixed together. The trade secret here is to add milk to it when the customer orders it. If the product is hideous, then you simply pour more milk in. I was quite good at this.

I'd sell it in any state, blaming everyone else for my misfortune.

The worst I ever sent out was totally separated. Totally. And it smelled like a barn.

It was for a take-out order.

This idiot woman wasn't supposed to check the product until she arrived home!

And then blame the dilapidated state of the product on her own driving. Simple.

Not worth going back for, and I'm a couple of bucks richer.

No harm done.

Unless she eats it, of course.

Eats. Drinks. Force feeds.

It brings a special warmth to my heart when I see customers out in the food court choking down the latest rendition of the chowder, too polite to come back. I usually go to the back and laugh.

The smell of this stuff makes me nauseous, but I always feign complete ignorance when a customer returns the "product."

I simply can't believe how this wonderful product has turned into "this" in a matter of minutes.

Impossible. No scientist or holy man could explain it.

Don't verbalize anything, just act completely dumb and make out like this is the first time you've ever seen this.

And I do another masterful performance.

Except the soup is so bad that her feelings are hurt. She thinks that I'm a bad person who's trying to poison her.

No I'm not. I'm counting on common sense prevailing and you throwing this slop into the garbage can, cursing on me a few times, and then returning to try your luck again.

"Thank you and come again," is serious.

This time I'm stupid enough to ask if she wants a replacement.

"Refund."

I look like the "Land of Refund" is on the other side of the world.

I now start to think of the potential trouble this lady could be, so I give her the money back.

I try to give her a faint look like now my kids will never go to college. And my mother needs an operation.

She's not buying it. Or the soup.

She leaves. I laugh.

My employees look at me in disgust. You mercenary!

Leave me alone.

I hate refunds. And chowder. And that "uncooperative" customer. And these "ignorant" employees. All useless commodities in the chain of "production"!

THE MALL RAT

Be gone with you all.

I never want to see another bowl of chowder in my whole life. Unfortunately, its putrid reek is engrained in my olfactory memory. Please help me.

I Let Him Do It

Who was my favourite employee?
Stan.
Stan was Willie Loman. The modern day Loser, who referred to his own being as, "My Little Bullshit Life."
He knew he was screwed.
Drop out. No real work ethic. No sense of money. His family was a mess, he had more ex-step-whatevers than you can shake a stick at. One of sisters turned 2 guys gay!
Reg couldn't approach Stan for the level of spiritual corruption. We used to joke that when Stan was born, his parents turned on the Playboy Channel and left for 2 years.
Not a moral bone in his body.
But you couldn't help but like him. Always in a good mood. The customers loved him. And although he broke just about every health code rule, he could cook.

And Stan had a special skill: he could instantly mimic anyone.
And I mean anyone.
Any kind of deformity or tick or habit or expression or saying or anything.

THE MALL RAT

If someone did it, he did it.

A lot of them were quite complicated, and he could do so many.

A generally "good hand" to have around. If you wanted something done, Stan would pitch in. Overtime, sure. If he was going to get coffee, he'd get you one. He was a non-stop chatterbox, and an entertainer worthy of Hollywood.

Stan was so funny. An A&W girl poked her head in one night and said, "First time I've been in here, whew, it really stinks." Stan: "Smells like your undies." He had perfect timing.

The laughs never stopped.

One morning, after a ménage-a-trois, the girl involved started texting Stan.

Ever one to kiss and tell, Stan shares the correspondence with me as she leaves home, gets on the bus, and journeys to the mall.

Stan is telling her to go away. He's working.

She's ready to go!

The last text before this creepy chick shows up reads, "BBQ?," in reference to some sleazy act performed the previous evening!

She doesn't realize Casanova here has been spilling the beans to the boss. When she gives him the Grade—B porn actress look I lose it and run to the back. He meets her later.

Yes, the fun never ended.

At least this was one of Stan's stories that was actually true. I saw it.

You see, to make up for Stan's slice of "quiet desperation," he had created a total fantasy world. Whatever he was telling you was usually absolute hokem. Absurd. Unbelievable.

He had more car chases than Burt Reynolds, more chicks than Gene Simmons, spent money like a tycoon.

And because he was so mentally quick (and believed a lot of it himself!) he could really go.

It wouldn't be uncommon for a customer to say something like, "You must be so proud of Stan!!"

"Why?"

"Oh, how he saved those 10 people in the burning building, performed skin-graft surgery on 2 of them, and went back and saved the old lady's kitty-cat."

He was something else.

Quiet Desperation vs. Fantasy World

But I was going to miss him.

He was going on to a career in changing tires. It paid more. He'd be out of debt in 317 years, instead of 617!

Now it was Stan's Last Day.

In a mean world, Stan was cheerful. And speaking of mean, look who turns up!

I can't believe it!

I hate this guy.

This is "Mr. Mouthy."

An argumentative, nasty 60-year-old guy who picks fights just to be a big mouth.

Whatever.

You never win.

And he always has bad comments on the food, but comes back every few weeks anyways.

And he's here.

Stan's finished for good in a couple of hours.

Gee, why am I thinking about a story Lyle told me?

Lyle and Stan were working one night and Stan was serving Mr. Mouthy.

They were talking about cars, Stan's favourite subject. Probably turned into some kind of pissing contest, and Stan slightly changed the subject.

"Took my car to the car wash last Saturday."

"Yeah. You should have left the windows down and got a wash. Look at that shit on your face, and your uniform is rotten."

I couldn't argue with the uniform part, (Stan left it at work every night. For 18 months) But the "shit" on his face was actually acne!

Stan was so hurt.

But hey, if you never wash your "uniform," and parts of it are actually eaten away, you may expect a negative comment some day! Picture Stan walking into Tiny Tim's Orphanage and the rats zipping it out the back door.

But what luck! Stan. This jerk. Bad blood. And food.

THE MALL RAT

It's perfect.

I didn't think twice.

I took Mouthy's order. I looked at Stan. Stan looked at me. Just for the twist I told him it was Stan's last day.

He didn't get it.

Stan cooked the fish.

When it was just about cooked he removed it, plated it, and smuggled it around the corner to the back.

When I rounded the corner, he had his fingers in his mouth and was applying his "secret recipe" to the fish.

He then tried to blow stuff out of his nose onto the fish.

This didn't really work, so he started to spit on the fish.

I finally told him enough was enough!

I could tell by his vengeance on the fish that he really hated this guy.

We served it.

Mouthy only snarled and said something negative. Stan smiled. He was happy as usual, after all.

I let him do it.

I had to.

Stan left a couple of hours later. We parted on good terms, good times to the end.

The last we heard of Stan he was building a mansion in another city. And he just had a testicle removed! And…

Stan. Stan. Stan. Good luck (Lo) Man!

I Gotta See This

If my tenure as fast foodie taught me anything, it's that we can safely assume the average level of civility is declining.

The good are better, the bad are worse.

You meet some really ugly characters. Abusive. Unsavoury. Unpalatable. Base.

One "lady" furnished me with a line I'll never forgot. I'm sure it wasn't her intention to give me an eternal laugh.

I'm at the cash register, waiting to serve my next happy customer.

"Hi. What can I get for you?"

"I don't want to buy anything. I just want to tell you you have the worst food I've ever had."

Then she turned around, unhurried, and walked away.

Why bother? You old sack of dirt.

But I laugh every time I think of it.

The meanness and bitterness somehow strike right at my funny bone. Go figure.

But only one person can hold the place of "Worst Customer Ever."

It's a busy Friday night.

THE MALL RAT

Looks like a loud, ugly Philippino woman has decided to take her 2 zombie teenagers to the mall.

They're coming my way.

Some people you take an instant dislike to. She's one of them.

Chawing away on the cell phone. Trying to talk to the zombies at the same time.

Where did you buy those clothes? Let's get it over with.

Now I'm in a 4-way conversation with her, the zombies, and whoever's on the other end of the line.

This is painful, but at least she sort of knows what she wants.

So it's 2 orders of fish-n-chips and a fish and shrimp. Combos.

The zombies scrounge up enough energy to tell me the drinks. Wow.

Remember, every order is verbally checked and double-checked.

She's looking at the pictures of fish-n-chips and fish-n-shrimp.

It's done. I don't like her. But it's done. She only dropped the cell phone once.

They disappear with the drinks and a few minutes later mama is back to get the food.

"Here you go. Enjoy your meal."

"Where's my calamari?"

"I don't know."

"Where's my calamari?"

"I don't know. You didn't order calamari."

"Yes, I did."

"No. You didn't."

Did I mention I don't like her very much.

So now I go through the old song and dance routine. Explaining something to a brick wall.

Well, let's see. It's not on the ticket, which was checked twice verbally. You know you didn't order calamari. You also indicated those 2 pictures, there isn't a calamari picture at all. And you carted away 3 drinks, there isn't a calamari combo.

Strike 3. You're out.

Now enjoy your meal and have a good life. Far away from me. Thank you. God Bless.

I think one of the zombies must have changed, er, its mind, and now wanted calamari. Or she did. Or the person on the phone 3 thousand miles away. Who knows.

I never get a chance to find out as her next line is, "You'd better give me what I want or I'm going to start shouting and making a scene."

In retrospect, I should have given her the squid. We were doomed anyway, but she'd be the final nail in the coffin.

But, in business, you can't afford to just throw stuff away. I'm not running a luxury hotel in Manila.

Besides, I'm a sucker for a free show. I'm the wrong person to say this to. I'm about to get a free show.

And the 2 stoners waiting for their munch look like they're in the mood for some pre-drinking entertainment. I laugh when I think of their faces.

She only waits a split second and can tell I'm not going to cave.

Remember, this is a Friday night, so the place is packed.

She starts ranting and raving.

This is cool! She's out of her mind!

Her story is that I'm some kind of bad thief who won't feed her kids.

She's really going. Her audience gradually grows. She's trying to get louder. She's the "Village Idiot."

One of the kids tries to rescue "Mom." He's used to this show.

I try to give her the food again with this condescending smile on my face. I know this will really set her off. Like a bomb.

"This isn't my food. Where's my calamari?"

"You didn't order calamari."

She blows.

Now she's like a mad woman in an asylum!

The stoners admire my ability to press her buttons.

The audience is thoroughly enjoying themselves. Unbeknownst to her, every time she turns around I do little facial accompaniments.

Mock horror. Mr. Innocent. Imitating her. Fright.

They love it.

She doesn't get it, but their "interest" fuels her.

I have a nice little rapport going with the crowd, but all things must come to an end.

THE MALL RAT

And this comes in the form of a security guard.
Security guard equals trouble.
So I instantly play the part of the aggrieved merchant. "Save me."
I overdo it a little, but the crowd loves it, and this security guard isn't going to catch on.
"Crazy Mary" continues on, now ranting at the security guard.
I'm so innocent. "Ma'am, your food is ready."
With a straight face.
This totally incenses her.
Soon she is actually going to attack me.
But the security guard interjects with a proclamation of banishment.
"I'm going to have to ask you to leave the mall."
Now she's in a state of craziness.
I've played them all like a fiddle.
He even has to grab her by the arm.
"Do you still want your 2 fish-n-chips and fish-n-shrimp?"
I'm that bad.
He escorts her out, she's still loud and obnoxious.
I don't miss a beat.
I look at the 2 stoners and say, "Go for it."
"Right on."
Like vultures they're divvy-ing up the booty. With their hands. Shoving it in their take-out boxes. They're so happy, though.

Like a bad smell, she comes back.
I don't think I want to be 50-something and hiding behind a pillar waiting for a security guy to disappear so I can sneak back in a mall!
And she heads for a coffee place and rants to them.
I love people who have not one shred of sense in them.
She thinks no one will call security if she's not right in our faces.
We wouldn't call security anyway. Even if the place was on fire.
Round Two anyone?
But she eventually calms down, and leaves.
That actually took a lot of energy and on a busy night I just want to finish up and go home.
It's an isolated incident.

To be the "Worst Customer Ever" you really have to put on a show. What energy.

Too much energy.

A couple of weeks later I receive a "package" from the mall. Under the Marketing Lady's signature.

Wow.

Our ranter was gone to a lot of trouble.

I guess she's Philippino, and somewhere in the property management's employment there's another, get this, Philippino.

So she writes a letter to him introducing herself as a fellow compatriot, and asks him to defend her, right or wrong, based on nationality. These people suck.

I'm not making this up.

She's shameless.

She even invokes the parenthood card.

It's sickening.

What's more sickening is that this has found its way to the Marketing Lady.

Four years into this business, and I've only had 4 or 5 serious customer problems.

And every one finds its way to this person who hates me.

Unjustly. Well, mostly.

And this time the ML has really topped herself.

She's fanned this out to 6 or 7 more company employees! People I don't know.

Memo after memo after memo.

All in my little "package."

This is over 5 ounces of squid and a crazy woman.

One of the memos is about how the security guard must have acted improperly. It goes no to say how they should undergo the "Best Program," whatever that is. Sounds like a boot camp. For mall gumshoes.

And the Marketing Lady wants an immediate reply.

I wait a few days.

I craft a letter. And recraft.

Finally I have a letter with not one negative word.

For that right tone of sarcasm, I act like I know what the "Best Program" is, and comment on all the good work it's done. I even offer to give a talk on the "Merchant-Customer-Security Triangle." Whatever that is!

I have lots of insights, you know.

I picture smoke coming out of the ML's ears.

I also ask her if I can write directly to all these employees who I've never met. Why should my reputation be so easily dragged through the muck?

ML says I'm not allowed.

OK, Mom.

I realize it's a losing battle.

She says she'll add my reply to the "file."

Shove your file up your ass, sister!

It doesn't matter anyway.

Ten new enemies have been created out of nothing. Mission accomplished.

Remember this one. It'll be the trigger.

Deepthroat

Minds out of gutter, please.
Deepthroat.
The Informant.
The One who sees that information can be provided to right wrongs.
And today I'll meet mine.

It's Lyle's birthday. He's off. I've let whoever was working with me go home ages ago.
It's well after nine.
It was a slow night. Slow nights make you draggy when you're cleaning up.
It's getting to 9:30.
Time to call it quits.
The lights are dimmed in the food court and in the halls. The food court has a huge glass ceiling and the colors and atmosphere are different at different times of day. It's a clear, hot summer night. Hopefully Lyle won't have too much of a hangover tomorrow.
Day's done.
I'm leaving the smelly room. Off go the lights, through the door I go.

THE MALL RAT

And now the worst moment of 63 months of ownership will occur!!!
I turn around to face a person I recognize. He works for the mall.
"Hey, how's it goin' ?"
"There won't be a Billy's in the new food court!"
"What?"
"There won't be a Billy's in the new food court."
"What do you mean?"
He repeats the sentence.
"How do you know this?"
He tries to speak.
No words come out.
He then promptly beats it, thinking he's made a mistake!
I think I slumped against the wall.
I know this heavy feeling came to the back of my eyeballs.
I couldn't really comprehend it.

My first thoughts were the quick calculations.
What's the bet on this person's credibility?
High.
How long does the patient have?
Twenty-one months tops. Depends, though.
In business terms, this is nothing. No time.
We end up staying exactly 1 year less 3 days! 1 year "exactly."
What do I do now?
This is a major, major day ruin-er!

And my mind quickly establishes the cause of my woes : The Marketing Lady.

Deepthroat is a "relative" of this Marketing Lady. Related department.

He's privy to information, at least information that's gotten through office politics and meetings. On the grape vine.

To this point in my recanting the tales of Billy's, I've finished 4 or 5 stories with "Remember this one."

"R.T.O." is akin to "Remember the Marketing Lady."

From Day One, to our demise, she's been waiting to pounce, and it's coming around.

Our lease is good for six more months.

The mall renovation plan says the food court will be moved to another part of the mall no later than 21 months.

We stay one year.

From the moment I laid eyes on this woman, there was nothing but trouble.

Her initial looks made me extremely wary.

If I ever had to talk to her, it was always with the utmost courtesy and respect.

If the mall sent a questionnaire, I answered it.

If they wanted a prize or coupon, I'd try to give them something.

Why?

To stay totally out of this person's way.

I never wanted to deal with this person at all, and I made sure every move was calculated.

But of course, it was downhill all the way. Aided by her refusal to ever deal with anything. All the paperwork would just go in her "file." And then she'd smile.

File means indictment.

And I did see this outcome occurring.

Again, I'd be so sweet to the mall people.

At the same time, I was praying her power wouldn't get larger. Or she'd move.

But of course it was downhill all the way.

Too many mall managers in too short a space of time. Her power multiplied!

So from the weatherman to the lady with dementia to the dancer who brought the security, to the loon who wanted calamari, our fate was sealed.

In her file.

I read her so easily upon first meeting her.

Like a book.

And people like this like to include you in their "story."

They see the world in zero-sum terms.

So people who are in some situation they deem to be better than their own are somehow taking something from them.

And they feel good when they do some pretty rotten things.
And this woman's probably done more than a few.
But they're misguided.
Bill Gates is rich. He didn't take anything from me. The Fed issued bags of bank notes just for him. Not me. I don't care.
Same with this kind of person.
If you want something in this world, go get it yourself. I'm not the cause of your problems.
See, it's really simple. Don't be a hater. The good vibe might attract more people to you. Give it a try.
Not this old piece of slunk meat.
So it's July 3. Happy Deathday to Billy's.

I float out to my car.
I keep trying to absorb what my ears have just taken in.
I'm numb.
Shock.
There's no way out of this one.
If you're a small businessman who's in the precarious position of being a renter in an asylum, you wake up every day with the same thought : What can ruin my investment?
And every time I run the possibilities through my mind, the answer is always the same : No one can ruin you except the landlord, and within this lies the Marketing Lady.
Why has the only possibility been answered?
That in itself speaks to the correctness of my perceptions.
I've met "Little Miss Empty Life."
It's sad really.
One Loser is going to cost other people so much.
Beyond the money and livelihoods, we have a huge customer base. A lot of whom we know as friends.
The landlords are by nature absentee, but the real fact of it is we do "almost" as much customer service as the customer service counter does. Me and my staff are the easily identifiable white people, so we have to cater to hundreds of requests, many from the elderly.
Oh well.

(To tell you how funny the customer service people are, I once went there to buy some kind of tickets. It was like 08:59:45. The girl said they weren't open yet, and abruptly turned around. Back on. Fiddled with some papers.

Literally 15 seconds later she turns around like she's never seen me before. "Can I help you?" I could have decked her.)

The rest of the evening is a blur.

Accompanied by copious quantities of cheap brew, my mind races through so many angles and scenarios.

I do contemplate taking her out. She deserves it. There'd be a suspect list as long as your arm. I've watched enough Cold Case Files to pull this off! I actually could.

And then I passed out. With visions of homicide dancing through my head!

Sleep on it.

Deepthroat did the right thing. Wherever you are, thank you. You are a Saint. A Prince.

I shudder at the prospect of going into this trap with my eyes closed!

The mall renovation is in full swing. The food court will move. You will not.

S.O.S. All is lost!

Good Night, Vienna.

Tomorrow will be another day.

Interlude

The nature of this book is such that few of the stories depend on each other.

A mall is a constantly changing landscape, and most "events" are short term happenings. Only stories pertaining to our lease really matter!

From Deepthroat and Circle the Wagons, I wish to only address matters concerning our demise. They're the funniest of all.

The final step into the grave is the next item on the agenda.

Undoubtedly, some of the stories you've already read do take place in Year Five, The Last Year, but they're independent entities.

"The End of the Line" was only a black backdrop to the normal goings-on. Stalkers kept stalking, the ghost-spirit kept right on doing whatever it was doing.

And you had to keep on trying.
That's hard.
And putting up the facade.
Billy's Fish-n-Chips, where "Tomorrow We'll Be Gone." Lead on.
Yes, the everyday kept on coming.
And for whatever reason I alter two things.

I don't know why.

As a protest? Relief. Screw it.

First of all, I never don the company shirt ever again. I don't know why. Out come the concert and beer shirts.

"Welcome to I Don't Care Any More. Whatdaya Want?"

The second change I make, and I don't know why, is that I never bother testing the fish batter "thickness" ever again.

This drives Lyle nuts. A little part of our success is due to my careful mixing of the batter. It's perfect. Lyle loves it.

And now, for some inexplicable reason, I'm just not doing.

Lyle's on me all the time for this.

But his thirty seconds of harping is less than the six or seven minutes required for perfect batter. You do the math.

And so the initial shock of Deepthroat has somewhat subsided. It's July, it's six to twenty-one to go.

It's going to take so much energy and planning to pull off something I have no interest in anymore!

The goal is to "Disappear into the Night."

A perfect failure.

Let's see how I do.

Circle the Wagons

It's July 4th.

Waky-waky time.

Of course my first thought was to play through last night's saga in a nanosecond, and ask myself if it really happened or not.

It did.

We're screwed.

And now I have to take some kind of action.

I have to get my ducks lined up.

It's like a Rubik's Cube. If this happens, I do this. If that happens, I do that. The outcomes are too numerous to totally plan for. There are probably a few I haven't thought of either. Don't worry, it's early in the day. By sundown my mind will have pretty much covered it, I hope.

Of what I will do there is no doubt : CIRCLE THE WAGONS. How I will do it is the question.

My mind works totally backwards.

And that's a good thing. Outcome first.

I start with 1 basic idea AND 1 nagging thought.

The basic idea is this : When the time comes, I want to disappear into the night. Not a word.

My nagging thought centers around Deepthroat.

For my little withdrawal to be as successful as possible, I'm now wondering if my dear little informant has informed anyone of our little conversation.

By anyone, I could mean anyone, because I don't want him telling anyone of our demise. The word will soon get around and we'll be screwed.

But by this "anyone" I mean anyone who's a co-worker of his.

A lease, is a lease is a lease. It's July 4. On Jan. 1 we have no cover.

But if Deepthroat opens his mouth to the wrong (any) person, than the Marketing Lady knows that we know.

That wouldn't change the outcome, but it would make the ride a lot rougher. She's going to be a real bitch anyway, but I need to pursue a dignified, orderly withdrawal. A successful failure. I'm going to have a lot on my hands, it's going to be a lot of work, and the least amount of interference and distraction will be integral. To my mental health.

So I bet on self-preservation and figure Deepthroat isn't going to rat himself out. He'd get fired.

But I also know that other people in the property management company know this as well. A certain number must. But I can't control them.

But I must plan.

I must now try to embrace the idea that no one on their side of the fence will tell anyone on my side of the fence. I want to believe this.

That includes suppliers and people I do business with, customers, my employees, Billy's franchise Office, and, I guess, people I know in the mall. That's a long list.

I know I can't control all of this!

But I will control what I can!

I make a neat little game out of figuring out who on their side knows. I make a short list and put these 3 or 4 individuals on my radar.

What I find truly amazing is that this actually works. I can't control who already knows, and I can't control the timing, but everything else I can influence.

And it starts with 2 things.

The first is that only 5 people will know : me, the minority shareholder, my father, my sister, and her husband. No one will breathe a word.

Incidentally, my sister always gave me interesting commentary on the Marketing Lady. She's worked in a business hierarchy, and would tell me why the ML was doing whatever she was doing. Her "file" was about building "evidence," forging alliances, and then steering everyone to her "outcomes" without any dirt or trace on her hands. In short, knowing how the system works.

I gave the other 4 all the information and we agreed there was no way out.

All I could do was make a plan to deal with everyone I had to deal with.

Secrecy would be critical, and I only informed people on a need-to-know basis. Sometimes even then I'd drag my feet for 48 more hours.

Outwardly it's business as usual. But I'm circling the wagons.

My suppliers and business associates?

They're only nuisances anyway. And a source of gossip. No need to tell them. Actually, when I do inform this group, they are all so sorry and pledge to help me at the end. Then they squirm out of it when the time comes. Human nature. No more money to make!

My employees? No. They're a huge possibility for leaks. And who wants to talk about this day in, day out? Not me. And there's a remote possibility they'll blackmail me in some way. No thanks.

Billy's?

The good old franchisor.

This is risky business.

If I thought they could actually help the situation, I'd involve them.

And that would mean an executive at Billy's would know someone important at the property management company, and would have sway with him or her. Like play golf together kind of thing.

I'm picturing the gang at Billy's, and not holding out much hope there.

If I've noticed anything about Billy's, it's the "Not my Job" attitude. In 4 years they've done so little for me and my store that it's laughable. Most of what they do is irrelevant at best, counterproductive at worst.

I feel if they get involved, this will turn into a disaster, more people will know, and nothing will be accomplished. To add insult to injury, I'll probably be "blamed" somehow. Me. The future "Franchisee of the Year"!

But I will subtly keep them informed throughout the process.

And the customers! Don't even go there.

There're probably a million people I want to get away from. Four years is enough. My nerves are frayed from the collective onslaught I face each day.

I can make it the rest of the way with my sanity intact if I go about it in secrecy. And I'm good at secrecy.

So, it's the five of us to the end.

Our first inclination is to quietly sell this turkey.

I laugh at this idea.

Who'd be dumb enough to buy a business with 6 month's worth of lease left, and the huge expense of a new store?

But I have to act in the best interests of the shareholders, and I'm one of them.

This idea soothes my conscience when it comes to suppressing the news from everyone. The law says I have to do what's good for the company. You know.

Anyway, it's good cover. Shareholders' Rights.

So I dutifully run an ad.

And I only get one response in like 3 weeks.

It's pitiful.

My lone respondent is a stunned East Indian named Bozo or Bonzo or something.

This is ridiculous.

It's so painful to deal with someone who's stupid, but not quite stupid enough to do what you want!

I try to sell the idea of a "new lease" like he's won a new car, but he's not buying it, and after I explain his good luck for like the 4th time, I hear a click.

It's a bad kind of click.

Click.

You're screwed.

So now we are back at Square One.

There's truly no way out.

Silence is working. It's business as usual.

The second thing is to be very organized.

THE MALL RAT

First, I make a mental flow chart of who and what has to be done when.

I eventually commit this to paper, with appropriate check lists and numbers.

I'm pretty good at this, and my initial list is about 90% complete.

It'll all unravel once humans get into the equation, but that's life.

For now, it's five people with a secret. There won't be any leaks.

We have a date with the executioner, that's all I know. In 6 months! In 21?

It hardly makes any difference.

It's going to be horrible.

You're in decline. Winding down.

This is going to suck.

At the end, I'll be in this place, alone, carting out the last wares from the place. It'll rain. All will desert you at the end.

Except Lyle. He's about the only helpful one I know.

So on we go.

I feel good about my initial response. Circle the Wagons. Remain Calm. Don't breathe a word. Hope for a miracle.

Start planning. The shock wears off. A multi-prong game of "denial" begins.

Deathrow

From the 4ty of July to the New Year constitutes half of our remaining time, although I don't know that yet.

The shock of Deepthroat has subsided a little. Just a little.

All my ideas developed over the last few sleepless nights are more or less cemented now.

We must accept that we will be booted out of the mall.

It's tough. The investment is gone. I didn't put much into it at the beginning, and thankfully most of the balance is paid off. But the value of this business is zero, not the hundreds of thousands it is worth on paper.

We must also proceed in secrecy and leave on a run out the back. I don't want to deal with any of it!

So I now have a square on my hands. My "realm."
One corner is my business associates.
One corner is the customers.
One corner is my employees.
And one corner is the franchisor, Billy's.

The business associates will only be informed of our demise at the last minute. No need to worry about them, or that I should take any action at all.

THE MALL RAT

They're on the back burner.

Ditto for the customers. I don't owe them anything in reality, and I don't want to have that stricken conversation 10,000 times. So they join my suppliers and business associates on the back burner.

Two down, two to go.

And these are the two I need to do a little preliminary work on.

The employees and the franchisor, Billy's.

Such is the mind-set of the condemned. Sit on Death Row clue-ing up the loose but inevitably "dead"-ends!

The employees are mostly easy to deal with. They're either part time or don't have that much seniority. I'll take care of them in any event.

I've always been good to them, so I'll look out for their interests to the end. They're a little part of my flow-chart.

The only employee of any real import is Lyle.

He was here before me.

He and I will be the last two on the Sunday night before the next dawn's execution. Every one should get loaded the day before the end. We did.

No one more loyal than Lyle. No one more comical, too.

He had the knack for the verbal gaffe. Yogi-isms. Lyle-isms.

One day, Lyle, an employee who speaks English as a second language, and an employee who doesn't speak English at all are "talking" about Gypsies.

Three of them.

The employee who doesn't speak English says she doesn't like Gypsies at all. She comes from Eastern Europe, so some wanderers must have sold her some watered-down vodka. Or cheap panty-hose.

It's hard to make any sense out of her at all, so soliciting opinions may not be time well spent.

I once tried to ask her questions about life back in the Motherland. I was enquiring about how many children she had and she thought I was giving her a food order.

She answered, "Combo?"

Oh, forget it.

It turns out she has a boy and a girl, so I guess that's a "combo."

In any event, talking to this woman about anything like Gypsies is useless. But that's OK.

Lyle's two-cents is, "Yeah, I don't like them either. They're not very friendly. They won't even invite you in their house."

"Hi, I'm a stationary gypsy."

Lyle-isms .

Some people have it, some people don't.

Some people really have natural comic ability.

Our original thinking was for Lyle to take over Billy's after I had no more interest in it.

Then it was take it over after we moved it to the new food court.

But now Lyle's thinking has changed.

Thankfully.

He has served his time. He's young.

He doesn't want to take over this problem-ridden place any longer.

I can't blame him. He's seen too much. He's in his early 20's and has seen more than most see in a lifetime! Five years of entertainment. Good and bad.

I'm not going to tell him about Deepthroat.

I want him to come to his own decisions.

If I tell him we're gone, he'll jump ship, maybe.

Or want more.

Or tell people.

Or debate the legitimacy of Deepthroat.

Or. Or. Or.

No influence from me.

So I give him the different scenarios, but inform him I'll want out too when we move and set up in the new food court.

I suppose there is some remote chance that this will happen.

Not really.

So we propose a percentage split based on my current knowledge of what'll be left in the end.

I go a little on the generous side. It's easy to give away clouds in the sky.

So it's decided.

I'm relieved.

If there is money left over, I'll share.

If not, no one's going to volunteer to settle the debts. If you get my drift.

That's life.

My conscience is clear, so my attention to my employees is not needed at present any longer.

Employees. Business associates. Customers.

All in neat little boxes in my mind.

Hmm. The Franchisor.

What to do?

If they can help us survive, OK.

But I'm not counting on them.

I usually have very little to do with home office.

I stay out of their hair, they stay out of what's left of mine.

But I do have to deal with them occasionally.

And during the fall I have to deal with them twice.

One is to renew my Franchise Agreement.

It renews at the same time our fictitious new lease comes about.

Five Grand.

In the toilet.

When I drop off the check, I have a really phony conversation with the management about future plans.

By this time the writing is further on the wall concerning our execution, so it's hard to part with my 5 G's. It's 5 G's or spill the beans!

I'm buying a ticket on the Titanic.

"Last call for the Titanic."

"Wait for me."

My second interaction with the home office is my attendance at the Annual General Meeting.

I went to this shindig once.

That was enough.

The hotel that hosts it has the best air-conditioning in the world. It took me hours to thaw after I left!

And the food was "inconsumable."

Not to mention the endless sales pitches. A lemon cutter for $250.00. Sure.

I'm freezing.

I vow to not waste my time again, even though the Worldwide

Headquarters for our company is only a short drive away.
So every year it's a different excuse.
"Sick staff" seems to be foolproof.
But this year the Regional Manager is really pushing me to attend.
I figure it's because attendance is really sagging. I couldn't imagine buying a plane ticket to come to this.
Even if it is in a big city.
My second impulse is that he wants me to take part in some practical joke.
Or they're going to play one on me.
By his pushiness I sense something is on the go.
I really try to weasel out of it, but he won't have it.

So I go to the hotel.
It's still cold.
And so the business meeting starts.
I'm sitting closest to the door.
And the big announcement is that we are now going to engage an advertising company, and try to be a real chain.
Starting with radio ads.
This guy gets up to give his pitch.
He has good credentials, and apparently he's going to rip-off a successful campaign he already has going. I mean use it as "inspiration."
Sounds good to me.
It's going to cost the franchisees a couple of percentage points, but it'll be worth it.
Let's move on and finish this boring presentation.
Hardly.
The "Irate Franchisee from Hell" now enters the discussion.
He's pissed off.
From 60 feet I can tell he has a roaring hangover.
And I surmise his business isn't going too well.
And he doesn't want to spend a dime unless we're "guaranteed" that this thing is going to work.
Did I mention he has a hangover?
This causes us to endure 10 to 15 minutes of illogical harangues.
Finally, he has nothing left to say.

I personally will not be around when the ads hit the airwaves.

(By the way, they were hokey. I'm glad I didn't have to withstand the customers' jokes.)

"Aar Captain, Eat Shit"

So now it's on to other business.

Coming up, it's the Franchisee of the Year Award.

Company big wig gets up.

Makes heart warming speech about the attributes of this year's recipient.

I look around to guess which one of these guys goes home with the faux-veneer plaque on the wall.

And the winner is…Me!!!!

"Come on up, Gary."

I want to scream. Or laugh.

But not tell the truth.

"Thank you."

I'll soon be leaving the happy company, so I might as well be gracious.

I exchange some words with the company owners before I leave. Nice people.

I laugh all the way to my car.

I laugh all the way back to the mall.

No one can believe I won something, which kind of hurt my feelings!

My feelings were further assaulted when everyone kept telling me how much they did to help me win the award!

This actually almost made me physically sick. I can only laugh now.

I won in spite of them all!

I've been dragging everyone along for 5 years.

So, I finally get my own piece of faux veneer. Small reward for all the shit I've put up with.

And they keep up with it.

Anyway, I never bother to mount it on the wall at the store.

It'll only be coming off the wall soon anyway.

And it'll be in better shape as a souvenir if Mr. Do-It-Yourself leaves this thing alone!

I have a box where I keep all the quirky souvenirs from jobs and businesses I've had. Hand stamps, entry passes, "recognition awards," and so on.

My favorite is a very sarcastic fax a businessman sent me asking why myself and another man stood him up for a breakfast business meeting in Taipei.

I was acting as an intermediary for my friend.

Well, the sad fact is we ended up in a traffic jam, and never made the meeting because Mr. McGoo here wasn't smart enough to allow for traffic. By the way, Mr. McGoo drives this route every day.

My enduring memory of this is being stuck in traffic, and listening to the 1812 Overture on the radio while I stare at our hotel destination miles over there. Hilarious.

So I've paid my franchise renewal fees and I'm Franchisee of the Year, so do you think these guys are going to help me if things aren't looking good with the landlord?

Not a chance.

I'm dealing with the employees. And the head office. And my business associates. And the customers are still getting a 100% effort from us. It's not their fault that this mall will play this dirty trick on me. One person will take it all away.

Head up. Keep moving.

And it's all in order. As far as I can tell.

But it's six months to the end of the lease, and I have to take some action with the landlord.

Unofficially, I'll try to gauge some of the mall employees to see what I can pick up off them. Their attitudes will reveal something. I know which ones, to some extent, are the Marketing Lady's little buddies.

I don't see much of the mall administration staff, but the looks they'll give me will tell me something.

The parent company, which actually handles the leases, is in another city. So I find out who is in charge of my lease and write him a letter.

I craft this letter to accentuate the positive, and of course not mention the negative.

The negative being you've probably been guided to a "future

termination" recommendation by our friends here at the mall.

Never underestimate the power of a schemer.

She can make this guy do whatever she wants, under the cover of some other seemingly perfect rationale.

No answer to my letter.

I phone the turnkey.

Now he's giving me the vacation excuse.

I hate excuses.

I hate accidents, too.

Excuses equal laziness. Accidents equal stupidity.

He'll be getting around to it soon.

When people have bad news, they procrastinate.

So I won't be hearing from Turnkey any time soon.

And the clock is ticking.

The closer to the end of the year we get a "new lease on life," the worse the terms will be.

Or maybe no lease at all.

We'll get a month's notice, so Nov. 30 now looms as a date with the executioner. I don't see how you could do the huge December business, and make all the withdrawal preparations. That's crazy.

Sometime in November an envelope arrives from the Landlord.

I have never looked at an envelope with such trepidation!!!!

Is it my Commutation? Or my Notice of Execution?

Well, it's a lease all right.

A 1-year with a 1-month termination.

We're gone.

They only want us here in conjunction with their reno plans. When the plan moves to whatever phase, they'll hoof us out.

Wring us out.

They even have the audacity to up the rent!

If the reno goes more than a year, they'll offer us another 1-year deal a year from now.

Check Mate.

I phone the man at the head office to confirm all the details.

I try to act like the mall doesn't have definite plans, and we're still in the mix.

Any planning questions and this man's voice will rise. He's lying.

And whenever he mouths negative words like "termination," his voice rises.

He's stressing. He's avoiding.

Don't work for the C.I.A. there, buddy.

I'm not sure how the Marketing Lady controls you, but she does.

Now I have a definite proposal in my hands.

Time to see what Billy's is made of.

We're in serious doggy-doo.

I phone the "powers that be" at Billy's and inform them of our new lease terms. I go to the Head Office to see what's what.

Time to get out the Rolodex and make some calls. Use some connections. Do something.

Of course I can't inform them of what I already know, but I have to prod them along.

This is only right.

All these management people get paid pretty well.

Time to earn some of that royalty money.

The Billy's people are nonplused. Non chalant. Non everything.

It's "Non Voyage" time.

Here's a painful lesson. The franchisor will almost never help an individual franchisee. Why? Because they deal with these huge landlords on a national level, and won't stick out their necks for little old you.

At the same time though, they're right there for the franchise renewal fees!

Human nature can be ugly. No doubt.

To these day, this little piece of the meltdown wrangles the other partner in our business.

As Managing Partner, I'd already seen firsthand, countless times, how inept and lazy they were. No news to me. It was just another in a string of events.

THE MALL RAT

Relations with the mall administration become more strained.

My "gauge the mall employees" will pay off.

One of the women who works for the mall now looks away when she walks by. She falls into the embarrassed category. She just doesn't want to even look at us. She knows what's going on for sure.

On another occasion one of the office underlings phoned me for a response to some nothing fax questionnaire or participation in some coupon deal. Or something.

Her tone of voice was scathing. Cat and Mouse (in corner). Cop and Bad Guy. Teacher and Errant Pupil.

I'm going to be mean to you.

I get it, sister.

The vibe is all negative.

I don't know why all these peons have such an interest in our downfall. I guess it's part of the pack mentality.

The funniest of these episodes concerned the so-called Building Engineer, Gray Rob.

There are good engineers, and bad ones.

The guys at the top of the class run our physical world. Big jobs.

The ones at the bottom become these "site engineers." Run a building or facility of some kind. Dust off the old textbooks every time you meet a new problem.

Gray Rob is one of these "Hail Fellow Well Met" types.

All the permanent contractors at the mall laugh at him behind his back. A couple of them laugh right in his face.

He's just coasting through this engineering gig, as long as he doesn't create disasters, he'll reach retirement day.

I don't like two-faced people, so Gray Rob isn't my cup of tea. A real ass-kisser. Confidante of the Marketing Lady. He knows for sure, but he acts all buddy-buddy to your face. He likes my staff discounts on food, so he'll show up and tell you how great you and your food are. Behind your back, it's a different story.

One morning I'm walking in through the south doors. It's 8:00.

Starbucks is open.

Gray Rob is in line with another man, who looks to be one of the contractors working on the reno project.

The Gray One sees me, whispers something to Mr. Contractor, who then wheels around on a dime and stares/glares at me.

I'm the only person there.

So what did Mr. Two-Face say to this person, who I don't even know?

Take your pick.

A. Go to Billy's, it's great.

B. See that guy, he's so cool. I wish he were my friend.

C. That's the guy we're throwing out. Can't wait.

If you guessed "C," then you were right.

It's a nice way to start your day, enduring the snickers of the prison guards!

So that's our situation up to Christmas.

We're on thin ice.

We can go anytime. One month's notice.

Those last words are the new reality come Dec. 31.

Deepthroat told you so.

All actions indicate our demise.

No one can help you.

Merry Christmas.

Oh, but the mall does have any early Christmas present for me.

It's called an "Audit."

An Early Christmas Present

I love early Christmas presents. That little taste of what's to come.
And, look, what do we have here?
It's an envelope from the mall.
At this point, any envelope looks like a live grenade!
The lines are drawn.
We're gone. It's only a matter of when.
Deepthroat has been a double-edged sword.
Knowing in advance will probably save me a heart attack, but keeping all these balls in the air has been hard. And will get harder.
Dealing with, looking at, or thinking about the landlord is increasingly not my scene.
Innocently looking at a person and trying to cull some meaning out of them is depressing. It's always the same. "We're a pack of (cowardly) wolves. But you're screwed."

And so I have an envelope.
I never open bad news on the spot, and wait for an opportunity when I'm all alone.
Whew!

I'm lucky.

I'm so lucky, my itty-bitty soon-to-be out-of-business fish shop has been chosen by the landlord's accounting firm to be part of a "Quality Assurance Questionnaire" kind of thing.

It's my lucky day!

This paper "herald" also informs me that more details will be forthcoming, and states the odds of your being chosen.

I can't believe they asked me. Little old me!

This smells like an audit or some other harassment.

Like Chinese Water Torture. First, a notice, then. Then. Then. Then.

It's a win-win for the Marketing Lady.

Bother and bill you.

I try to see what Confucius' reaction to this is.

That guy is so smart.

Just a whiff of the letter, and he connects the dots. The conversation gently shifts to what I'm planning to do in the reno period. Very subtly.

The pupil can sometimes be as good as the teacher, and I subtly take the conversation somewhere else.

But he knows.

And he tells me it's nothing good.

It happened to him at another mall.

So he really knows.

He's had quite a few businesses, but he's retiring at the time the food court moves. Like me, he'd like to sell this millstone, but can't.

All situations are different. His is spending more on a business than you can sell it for.

So they make me wait for a couple of weeks.

Then more correspondence arrives.

And a call from an accountant at their accounting firm, located in another city. It seems "Little Missy" here will be in town on this particular date, and would I kindly have this, this, this, and this, in this particular order, for her at this particular time.

Since she's coming from out of town, I ask her where she'll be examining these 3 or 4 boxes of papers.

THE MALL RAT

No answer on that.

I sense that detail hasn't been worked out.

But since I have quite a bit of experience in business, and I'm talking to some recent college grad, I persist.

Why?

Well, records examined in some less than secure environment tend to have things spilled on them, looked at by prying passing eyes, or even stolen if unattended.

Never heard of it. It wasn't in our Accounting 401 class!

I don't tell Little Missy my concerns, only that I hope the mall, a landlord by the way, has space for her for that day!

The express purpose of this little audit is to make sure we've been reporting accurate sales numbers.

Our sales numbers are not even approaching the level to pay extra rent.

I'd love to pay extra rent. It would be my honor!

It's called "Percentage Rent." Please, please.

So this is totally a waste of time.

Part of this game is to let you know that your time is being wasted.

So I prepare the 4 boxes of material.

I'm a very good record keeper, so while the Marketing Lady envisions me pawing through shoe boxes of receipts, I just take them off the shelf, and finger through them. Yep, all there.

A few days before the audit, our recent college grad phones me to tell me that only 2 of the boxes will be required.

I remind her that you'd need the 4 to audit, 2 won't do it.

She brushes that aside. She's an "Accountant," you know.

I ask her again where her office will be, so that I can deliver the "records" to her.

No answer.

It will be my day off, but I assure her that it'll be no trouble at all for me to do that.

She just tells me the time she'll be around.

On the appointed day, she shows up on time.

She's pleasant enough in an "I'm a real bitch" sort of way.

I'm in a hurry, but pretend not to be.
I enquire yet again as to where my records are going.
She just takes off with them.
I leave.
When I return, the boxes are there.
My staff informs me that she babysat the boxes in the food court!
In the food court!
Around substances, wandering eyes, and thieves.

I knew she would.
This "accountant" apparently gazed at some of the papers for 30 minutes and then returned the boxes. And left.
I just laugh at all this.
This "look at the records business" is just a screen for something else.
And the laughs continue.
The accountant's report to me is hand-written on the back of a travel itinerary! A computer printout travel itinerary! I'm serious.
Maybe this accounting firm is fictitious as well!
Her "recommendations" are meaningless, akin to telling someone to stand up straight and wash behind their ears.
Total nonsense.
But I'm glad it's over.
Hopefully I never hear from this again.

But of course I will.
It's a bill. From the mall. And a letter.
Apparently, the auditors have found that my company has violated a subsection of the lease calling for the submission of an audited master cash-tape each year.
And because I have violated this sacred covenant, I am obliged to pay for the audit!
If you are confused, don't feel stupid.
I know it's hard to make all the connections. Particularly between the 2 boxes of records and this mysterious cash tape.
Also, enclosed, is a copy of the auditor's report, and I'm not making this up. Little Miss College Kid said that I was pretending to be sick, and that I

was uncooperative! And that was about it. A few lines about call Mom on Sunday and so on kind of thing.

It's like a "Tunnel of Tormenters" at a theme park.

It's so in-your-face, and obviously meant to insult your intelligence.

Like everything else though, I see the humor in it, and laugh at it.

This is how it will go.
This is your little mission.
These are your flunkies.
You see this is the nature of people like the Marketing Lady.
Married people do things with their families in the evenings.
Single people like you, disgruntled, angry spinsters, don't fill in their time that way.
They have time to hover over their laptops, read leases, go to their office, check files, and make plans.
They focus their discontent on some imaginary foe, a zero-sum game where this person's good life is because of your bad one. They took it from you. Revenge!
Be the happy old spinster, like the ones sadly generated by World War 1. They were happy and productive people.
Not like this crowd.
They're nasty and evil. And have jowls and thighs. And fake blond hair.
It's actually funny to look at the lives you intersect with over a lifetime. Some good, some bad.
This one's bad.

And of course since I violated your precious lease, I have to pay the bill for the audit!

I think they'll rob me for $300. No, up it to $500 because they are sickeningly greedy.

The bill arrives.
It's $1,050!
I'm not kidding.
This comes under the signature of someone I've never heard of.
So I phone him.
He promises to fix it but I never hear from him again.

The reason is simple.

As a tenant, you have money with the landlord.

They're simply going to deduct the money you "owe" them from your final statement. Or somehow get it.

Returning your call or giving you an explanation is simply a waste of their time.

And besides, the audit bill will only be 1 of a list of phony charges on your Final Account Statement.

Money with landlords is money you'll never see again.

That's why they consistently rank on the list of Least Admired Jobs.

Funeral Directors. Used Car Salesman. Insurance People. And Landlords.

So this is the run-up to Christmas.

We're toast.

And in a few short clicks of the calendar we'll be slowly walking to the chair.

It's a month to month lease from Jan. 1 onwards, so everyday is a bad day, so to speak.

I wonder which day will be the day.

But at least I got this early present. From being "a chosen one" to paying $1,050, all in one package.

Merry Christmas!

The Last Rites

The Last Rites.
The Last Wrongs, I guess!
Christmas comes and goes.
The painful long-term mall reno inches along.
It's a New Year.
Customers are talking about the reno more and more.
Just general stuff.
Their lack of familiarity with the situation makes their comments largely irrelevant. But their naïve views of business are fascinating.

To be fair, though, even some of the business owners themselves weren't dealing with reality. One guy thought the mall was going to buy us all new stores! And the same owner asked me how much the mall was paying to have our stuff removed! A real slap stick guy.
This is just hilarious.
And this is what starts to make the condemned man feel better.
He realizes that actually moving to the new food court will result in an even bigger money loss.
That's right.

They are now starting to "negotiate" with the various tenants.

And the terms put you into shock!

Our rent would have gone from 88K to 188K.

Plus 200-300K for a new store!

The mall even wants a 25K "contribution" from each tenant for common-area furniture. It's insane!

It would be easy for me to have a business that could be sold for less than what I'm putting in!

Getting out at zero looks good now.

And sooner than later, too.

The landlord is stealing a quarter of million in net worth from everyone.

And now there'll be 3 businesses out of 14 making a profit, instead of 12-13.

You are now working for the mall!

For nothing.

If you sell, you will lose.

It's nuts.

You start with a general store, you get Wal-Mart.

Same progression in malls.

You start renting space from them, no questions asked.

Forty years later they're into your company books!

Everything is reported.

They have perfect information.

On how to enslave you!

We actually "started" last in the food court rankings, and have been at 9 or 10 out of 14, and we are usually 11. Every one of the other food businesses will go to the new food court. Except us.

So I'm starting to see the benefits of our demise.

I start to sleep better.

One of the views held by the general public is that all the tenants are the same. One monolithic group.

Fourteen food joints, all moving in unison overnight.

Really there are 14 different stories going on, based on things like length of lease, clout of parent company, and so on.

The chicken place has 7 signed on years left of a 10 year lease.

It cost them 250 to build the store, and it's lost money all the way down the line.
They've tried to sell it from Day 2.
And the mall can make them move, sinking the same sum again or more!
That's totally insane.
Even the best case scenarios are depressing.
And reno traffic is slow traffic.
Next Christmas everyone will work hard for nothing.
And the time quotient also weighs on my mind.
From here it's anywhere from a one-month notice to a maximum of 15 months in limbo.
Mercifully, it is only 6 months.
Time is now being wasted at this joint.
You can get a lot of things done in that time.
I value time more than money generally, so this aspect of the deal gives me some anxiety.
It's done. No upside at all. Finishing my sentence. I get the feeling that I just want this to be over.

There's no crisis day to day.
Everyone's in the dark.
The only person even privy to our month-to-month lease is Lyle, and he only sees what he wants to see.
And that is a pot of gold at the end of a rainbow!
Be careful me son, the Mall Leprechauns are hiding under the escalators!
I have all the angles covered.
My little initiative of trying to gauge the mall personnel's vibe is paying off.
Although I'm unhappy to report that it's all pretty much negative.
And funny.

It's at these times that I give thanks for the enormity of Deepthroat's Gift.
Otherwise, all this would be going on under my nose and behind my back, and I'd be the sheep to slaughter! Actually, it's more like "up my ass" I suppose!

And I knew that Deepthroat would never rat himself out.

He walked away from me that night wondering how even he could be this stupid.

And he buried his little career-ender out in the parking lot of his mind somewhere.

Gray Rob's never liked me.

So he's an informed bystander.

He likes the "fact" that I don't "see" any of this coming. Human beings can be plenty nasty.

His little performance at Starbucks was the canary in the coal mine.

Thanks for the tip, Ace.

And now he's standing at my counter.

It's a Sunday afternoon.

Have I ever mentioned how much I hate Sundays?

Well, here's reason number 1018.

Gray Rob.

Splurging on a Sunday for a discounted fish dinner for he and the missus.

And he has this idiotic look at his face.

He's getting a charge out of the fact that the pie is soon going to hit me in the face, but I don't know it.

And it makes him feel happy because he doesn't like me. He admires the ingenuity of Big Mama in the office, and how he can enjoy this from the sidelines.

"Are ya ready for the Big Move?"

Wow.

Gray Rob has turned into a movie director, and he's just delivered his lead-in line to the gullible rube.

Now the gullible rube should say something like, "I can't wait. I wonder where our stall will be? I'm planning all the time, and my life has no meaning without this mall." Hick, hick, hick.

Then Gray Rob can walk away with his discounted food, snicker at me, and tell all the insiders tomorrow morning at the water cooler.

With no emotion, no anxiety, no aggressiveness, I say, "From what I gather, it doesn't look do-able. I haven't decided what to do."

It's a perfect performance.

I'm not that worried either way.

THE MALL RAT

Now take your fuckin' fish and leave.
Bye.
But I'm so cool about it.
You want a certain reaction, but you won't get one. Period.

One of the Marketing Lady's underlings provides me with a "Top Ten All-Time Look At You" memory.
It's at times like this that you wonder what's in some people's heads!

It's inside the mall.
In a corridor.
A long corridor.
100 feet long.
7-8 feet wide.
And here she comes, Little Miss College Bitch.
With a friend.
Obviously leaving the mall on some personal business.
They're in their mid-twenties and evidently looking for husbands, as the tenure of their rather loud conversation indicates.
"Ya. And he thinks he can be my man."
And she has this total bitch look on her face.
I gingerly approach them with this stupid, friendly grin on my face.
She then stops.
Her friend stops.
She then turns to me, HISSES like a cat or feline of some kind, and then walks on.
With her friend.
HISSES!
HISSES!
Really graphically.
You're crazy.
I don't need this.

Gray Rob. This chick.
Might as well have a paths-crossing with "The Thing from the Green Lagoon" herself!

I intersect her one morning at the top of the escalator.

My path and timing make me see her coming up into view for 3 or 4 or 5 seconds. Eternity.

I'm with someone.

She's not.

She literally walks through my personal space with not one hint of an expression.

We are the only 3 around, as it's about 10:30 am in this deadbeat mall, but she really acts like she's the only one in this large space.

It's quite an impressive performance.

THE WIND OF YOUR MOVEMENT BRUSHED MY BODY, yet we weren't even there!

Bravo, my Vindictive One.

You're just one of those people I must know in this lifetime. I'd sooner not, but that's the way it goes.

And the frontline office staff throw off the bad vibe as well.

Time for another episode of the Mall Annual Meeting.

I attended once. Once is enough.

But I'm polite, and businesslike, and so on, so I phone the office to R.S.V.P. my negative but friendly response to their Invite.

And the secretary is almost openly mocking me on the other end of the line.

Of course you're not going. We're kicking your ass out of here. Ha, ha, hick, hick, hick, ha, ha.

You must be dignified while you're suffering your indignities!

Strike number whatever. Yawn, yawn.

This hate vibe is getting old.

Spring'll be here soon.

Everything is moving along, but I daydream about being finished with this whole scene.

My disappear-out-the-back-door scenario is still intact.

Everyone's either in the dark, or held at arm's length.

And I want to get away from all kinds of people!

And then kickback for a while, far away from this place.

Bliss.

And now my phone rings.

I should have figured that the landlord wouldn't even be able to follow their own rules, either.

Why would they?

It's the leasing guy at head office somewhere.

"This is a heads-up call. In 30 or 60 days we're giving you the 30-day notice."

So it's the end of March. At the end of April or the end of May, you'll be either be leaving the end of May or be informed at the end of May for a June 30 Sayonara.

The end of May is my birthday, so I'm sure it'll be a good one this year!

Mr. Leasing guy's voice is all over the place.

I'm losing patience here as he babbles on.

I'm also in an extreme state of shock!

Although I've known this for an extremely long time, 9 months now, I'm still in shock.

Moving from percentage number 99 to number 100 is a little different than moving from say, percentage 37 to 38.

And I'm angry. At this person's dishonesty.

I'm sure this babbling idiot has axed a thousand tenants, but today's performance is really poor. The real word is stupid.

I don't like Mr. Nobody here controlling the conversation.

So I tell him I was informed by Deepthroat. I even give him the date and tell him to stop wasting my time.

"This was my decision alone," he asserts.

"Sure it was. That's why I knew about it ages ago."

"Impossible."

There's a good chance that he's just following "orders," and/or has no idea why he's doing what he's doing.

Anyway, this conversation is now useless, so I sign off.

I'm numb.

No illusions from this point on.

In 30 days we'll get a 60-day notice, putting our bums out on the street on June 30.

At least it by-passes the Condemned's birthday.

On my birthday I relive some of the great birthday's of the past. For a few minutes anyway.

I have a string going. I haven't been in my home city for about 20 birthdays in a row.

Some great ones. Camping by the Dead Sea. A really cool day in Rome. Feted to an extravagant meal in England, 2 cases of wine for that one.

Those people in Bristol were so cool.

I was visiting by "girlfriend association."

The host's brother, who was Keith Moon's brother, separated at birth, took me on a Pub Crawl.

Roaring drunk, screaming down these little roads in his Beemer. It was cold, windy and rainy. I'm in England.

The trees were hanging over the road.

And then "SWOOOOSHHH."

This huge tree, 60 feet by about 2 ½ feet in diameter crashes a few feet behind us!

That sound is forever in my mind. I physically feel it.

This guy once hopped up on a stage somewhere in Asia and joined in a nudey show. "I had to show them who was Boss."

Anyway, this birthday isn't going to be one of those.

It's going to really suck.

I'm going to be here working at the "Titanic Fish Stand," with icebergs up ahead.

At some point Lyle remarks that I won't be here this time next year!

I don't know whether to laugh or cry.

I'm days away from telling him that we're leaving!

But I can never bring myself to tell him all I know.

No Deepthroat story on his birthday.

No recounting of my plans.

No telling him that the Landlord informed me 30 days ago of our date with the demolition crew.

I just can't do it.

Lyle was here before I bought the place.

It's been the best 5 working years of my life.

THE MALL RAT

And that's why Lyle stayed. It was so much fun.
And one delusional woman is going to take it away.
That's life.

One week before the writing of this story, I ran into a former customer at a downtown office building.
"And I came around the corner, and you weren't there."
Yep.
And thousands like him,
Well, hundreds anyway.
And that will be that.
My financial downside will be minimal.
The employees are out of a job.
The chain will have one less outlet.
And the suppliers can supply someone else.
And I'll be in "Disneyland," if I can survive the next 30 days!

A Month of Sundays

One month.
It's going to be a blur.
Somehow, by the grace of God, my plan is working.
I'm 30 days from disappearing out the back door!
Everyone is pretty much in the dark.
Soon I'll be informing my lawyer, accountant, and the franchisor.
The first 2 can't talk anyway.
When I inform Billy's of our demise, they express no feeling of any kind. It's as if I'm telling them last night's baseball scores.
"Oh well, nice known' ya. Good luck."
And I'm the flippin' "Franchisee of the Year"! I can't believe it!
They have to deal with these landlords on a national level, so in their scheme of things it's your tough luck.
The customers are in the dark.
Suppliers and all people involved in our move will be informed 10 days prior to D-Day.
That only leaves the employees.
I'll tell Lyle now, although even that takes me days to actually do.
The rest of the employees will only get the 2 weeks by law.

The only unforeseen crack emerging in all of this is that the other food court owners are in full-swing negotiations with the landlord, and one way or another they're getting the idea that Billy's is out.

This is problematic.

One of them even starts to trick Lyle into divulging our status.

I now start to avoid all business owners!

If I see anyone coming, I disappear.

If I disappear, I don't have to talk to them.

No talk, no fishing for information.

That's it.

If I don't admit to anything, it doesn't technically exist.

And then I disappear out the back door.

No more customers, mall people, stalkers, ghosts, cross-dressers, and general weirdos.

It's all very simple.

These owners are pests, one lady in particular.

It's written all over her face that she knows.

And she thinks we're friends, so she's hurt that I don't confide in her.

She provides a comic moment, when one of my non-English speaking employees asks her for a job with about 4 days to go!

Idiot.

Yep, my fear of telling the employees was well founded!!!!

I spent more energy explaining how we weren't going to tell anyone to these folks than in any other task in our demise!

For sure.

Lyle's response to my news was, "When can we start telling people?"

Exactly. This is why I kept it all to myself.

Unexpectedly, Lyle was happy to get the news.

He was tired of the constant grind of Billy's, and the thought of being here for another year, profit or not, was too much to take.

I didn't expect this, but it made me feel somewhat better.

Lyle would be the only loyal one right up to the end. He really comported himself well. And we had as much fun as ever. In the last week, Lyle would be witness to our ghost pitching a steel rod off the cooler. He was there both times, actually. So Lyle's "Billy's Experience" went on to the end.

And so at least we were all happier!

But I had to reinforce the gag rule-news block out. Constant reinforcement. Constantly giving the employees yet another reason to shut their mouths.

The non-English speaking Russian lady was the hardest to keep in line.

We just couldn't get the idea across to her.

This is the same lady who, when asked how many children she had, replied "Combo?"

Of course when there are no visible signs of us leaving with about 4 days to go, she freaks and asks another food court owner for a job!

Idiot.

I'd already falsely promised that I'd find her a job at least half a dozen times!! Ingrate.

With war-planning like precision, I'd hung over the calendar with her, painstakingly spelling everything out, even this fairy-tale job across the food court somewhere.

Actually, I had about 3 different options on the employment angle, including the person she's now talking to.

I'd done my best. I even invoked the story of Potemkin. I think she understood the story, but not its relevance to our present situation!

Miraculously, she was the only leak. I was waltzing out the door and people were asking, "Are you leaving?"

If she'd shut up, I would have pulled this off perfectly!

In answer to Lyle's enquiries about "when" we were going to tell the customers, we finally negotiated telling 2 customers!

In the last week. If at all.

This wanting to tell people idea troubles me.

My mentality is exactly the opposite.

I never tell anyone anything.

Except what I want to.

So every human I know has some "view" of me. A slice. And I keep it all straight. Like you do.

Only St. Peter has the whole picture, and I'm hoping to slip by him hiding under one of those nuns' habits!

One of the people we'll tell is an old couple who "dine" with us 2 or 3 times a week.

And the other is this lady who brings her husband in his wheelchair/bed movable apparatus every week to eat with us.

This is their weekly treat, a little trip to enjoy a fish dinner.

She's young, in her forties, and the husband had a very major accident.

Caring for this type of person is a complete life's devotion, and she's tired and living frugally.

I never charge her. This saves her a grand a year, and costs me $300. I have a couple of "customers" like this. They deserve it.

And I don't want her to venture out with her husband to go to a place that doesn't exist any longer.

Luckily, both parties are informed in the last week, and go about their business without informing anyone.

I can't believe I'm getting away with this!

All suppliers and people who have to remove or de-install equipment are notified 10 days in advance. By fax.

The person who actually handles the fax is 2 or 3 degrees away form me, so even the food delivery people are in the dark right up to the last!

I'm very lucky.

Meanwhile, back at the farm, we just go about business as usual, although we start to use "See you next time" too much. Then we break into laughter. Bye Bye customers. And all the other baggage. When Lyle phoned me with the latest ghost story, all I could think of was how happy I'd be in a few short days.

I'd run a long race. A marathon.

It would be almost a year to the day since Deepthroat spilled the beans that we'd be leaving. 362 days. Or was it a Leap Year?

No more customer complaints, monthly reports, stalkers, floods, or the Marketing Lady. See ya.

Elvis is leaving the building.

And he can't wait.

Swan Song

It's Saturday morning.
This is the last official day of business!
Monday at midnight everything must be gone!
Of course it will.
And it's a nice sunny day.
And all the staff will be here.
I've told them how much fun it's going to be on the last day.
This is just a ploy.
I want to leave this dump a.s.a.p.
I've got a lot of drinking and work to do!
It's such a release of tension, I can't describe it.
With minimal security breaches, I've managed to pull off my sneak out the back door routine!
I can't believe it.
I try to figure out the mathematical odds, and I can't.
I'm just "PLAIN F_CKING LUCKY."

And now I want to get loaded.
And play through everything that will have to done in the next 62 hours and some odd minutes.

THE MALL RAT

It's been a rough week.
Lyle and I have been letting off steam by watching Clint Eastwood movies and drinking lots of cheap beer. Lots.

And right up to the end I'm the fly on the wall.
I'm entering the Blockbuster parking lot and I see Bono. It's like 10 p.m.
I'm dropping off another stellar Clint Classic and I see him eyeing a group of Asian youths.
I know what he's doing.
He's looking for a girl he stalked for a long time in the food court.
She lives 10 minutes from where he's standing, but he'll never see her again. It's a sad world sometimes.

Our ghost was active this week.
But I really no longer pay attention.
This ghost presented far more questions than answers, so short of leveling with me in a "Hi, I'm John Q. Ghost" sort of way, I'll never learn what I want to!

And it's been hard to get a decent night's sleep.
Not a dream, not a nightmare, but let's call it an "image," of one of my primary stalkers appeared while I was "asleep."
This is common.
Someone you know from everyday life doing something or other.
This is a "glimpse dream," a one-off image in your mind.
And this girl's face is screaming, angry, devilish. The scream doesn't stop. And her other features like her eyes are crazed.
It's quite disturbing.
But not surprising with a year's tension in me.
Oh well.
That doesn't bother me. No. No.
What bothers me is at the moment I awake from this evil woman, the 4 ½ long plastic lens over the lights decides to come crashing down on me!
Lucky again, I'm a person who awakes instantaneously.
I see it as it's leaving the ceiling and I manage to get my arms up in front of my face to shield and deflect it!
I'm drained.

I don't need this anymore.

And it's a nice Saturday in June.
Prime beer weather.
I think I make it to about 11:30 before I give in and start throwing back the beers.
I have no intention of serving any customers today. Perhaps the last few just to see who they are.
And to say, "See you next time."
I'll let the staff serve the remaining 200.

But before we get into the day's festivities, we might as well start the day with a coffee, and we send Lyle's brother over to get it.
A few days ago I found out that this coffee shop is going out today, as well.
All the Artists' Renderings of the reno that I've seen have Starbucks plastered everywhere.
One of the ploys malls use to make money is the idea of "exclusivity."
We'll give it all to you at a price.
The big boys in things like coffee do this.
We know they're finished today, but they don't know this about us.
So Lyle's brother goes over and orders.
They've always had a strange attitude towards us, and today is no different.
"Today's our last day. You're gonna miss us."
"Yeah. We're goin'. And you're gonna be here alone."
Don't flatter yourselves, ladies.
And with perfect timing he says, "It's our last day, too."
I laugh every time I think of it!
They're in shock.
I go over to them before I leave for the beer store, and tell them how happy I am. I genuinely am.
They're all bummed out.
They like working in this soap-operatic place with all these young women.
I don't.
I'm happy to be cutting out.

THE MALL RAT

I spend Saturday on the lamb, phoning once in a while.

I try to make it look like I'm going over there, but I'm not.

I'm running my plan through my mind.

At closing tonight, I'll count the inventory, and Lyle and I will empty the fryers and clean the equipment.

Any excess time tonight will be spent taking out small wares and so on.

Tomorrow morning, Sunday, I'll transport the inventory to a nearby Billy's before any workers come to the mall.

I know everyone's routine, so as long as I'm not doing this past 10 a.m. or so, I'm fine.

When the mall opens at 11, we'll be in darkness. Sort of.

Tell people it's a malfunction. Sorry for the inconvenience.

The auctioneers arrive at 2 to take all the equipment.

When all the equipment is gone, the counter and signage will still be there, so it'll look like a business. Potemkin's Fish-n-Chips.

The mall will close at 5, and our demo-crew arrives at 5:30.

One of Lyle's relatives is a general contractor, and he's coming to demolish the place. He can do all the electrical, plumbing and carpentry, so I'm counting on him big time.

On Monday, I'll be waiting around for Coke and couple of other people to pick up things, drop off the keys, and exit Stage Right.

Most of the suppliers and people I'm dealing with are so incompetent that I'm being forced to phone them, then fax them, and then mail the fax for insurance!

And they still manage to make a mess of it.

But it's Saturday, and the warm rays and cold beer give me a nice feeling.

I return at 7 for the last hour.

Everyone's happy.

We were actually busy and nobody cared about the work.

"See you next time."

"Come Again."

I get out there for a few customers, but I'm kind of inebriated.

Our stereo system will soon be beaten off the walls, but for now it's on bust as we count off the last few minutes.

Ten to eight.

Five to eight.
Eight.
"See you next time."
I think Lyle's brother called me a jerk.

We drink a few beers and wait for all customers and staff to leave.
Then we leap into action.
The inventory gets done.
The fryers are emptied.
Every single item in the place, now only has one question over it—"Where's it going?"
Lyle & Co. are really helping me out.
No one else will.
It's Saturday and by Wednesday 2 or 3 of us will be driving to California on a future-planned, but now spur-of-the-moment trip. No Disneyland. Redwoods.

Lyle's there on Sunday.
I arrive early Sunday morning and get rid of the inventory. It takes 4 trips. Lyle helps me out.
Our cleaning continues.
Luckily, Sundays aren't too busy, so we don't have too much explaining to do.
If I see some persistent type, I'll have a mouthful of beer, make up some imaginary mechanical problem, have another mouthful and continue working.
It's the afternoon and all's well.
Lyle leaves for a while. He'll be back with his demo crew later.
I'm dreading this.
I'm one of those people who thinks that there'll be some monumental screw-up somehow. We find the crew drunk in a bar, or whatever.

Meanwhile, the auctioneers are here to take away all the equipment we've been cleaning and disconnecting.
Auctioneers are scum.
Auction sounds sexy when you have a Monet to sell!

THE MALL RAT

But when it's used restaurant equipment, it ain't the case.

We're dealing with a bunch of thugs.

And the esteemed auction house gets us "S.F.A." for the equipment. A quarter of nothing!

I actually would have given the stuff away to someone to help start a restaurant. I really would have.

Luckily, they are in and out in literally 5 minutes. Wham, bam, scammed you man!

Anyway, I have bigger fish to fry. Well not really, anymore!

This demo involves all aspects of contracting work- carpentry, plumbing, and the dreaded electrical.

Plumbing's bad enough. I can write a book on all the plumbing escapades.

But I'm dead scared of electricity.

Especially in really thick cables.

Which obviously means I'm drinking more and more beer.

And this place is emptying.

It's kind of fun to just watch all the action in the food court one last time. Talk to a few people. The beer is making me confess our demise to a few people.

It doesn't matter now anyway.

Twenty-four hours from now I'll be gone. No midnight for me, I hope to go by early afternoon. But we'll see.

Right now I'm praying the crew has all the right tools. And back-up plans.

At last I hear the mall-closing announcement on the P.A. Yeah, thanks for coming.

I have this timed so that all mall traffic will be out of our hair.

It's going to be messy. And loud.

Well, we have quite a festive crew and the cooler door opens every 2 seconds.

But they work with zeal. Like Viking marauders. They know what they're doing and seem to like scrapping things.

Lyle and I are standing around talking and drinking when a huge piece of something goes by us. Out the door.

And more.
And more.
And more.
When the counter leaves, Billy's is officially dead.
Just one huge syrup slick where it used to be!
One giant caramel-colored sticky mouse trap!
No mice, of course.
They're next door having a Mama Burger. I'm serious.

They're ruthless. The workers I mean!
The place is gutted in 2 or 3 hours.
Time for the sign to come down.
My fear of electricity is lessened by the amount of beer I've consumed—I now have complete confidence in everyone.
Down it comes.
We attack it like a statue of Saddam Hussein!
Our company's logo is a huge fish.
This one is 2 or 3 feet in diameter and made of Styrofoam. It's a big head only.
I want it as one of my quirky souvenirs, so Lyle and I lay the boots to it until it surrenders.
This stupid fish cost me a fortune.
I take another mouthful of ale.

The crew is about done.
Scorched earth.
Just the hood fan and a couple of pieces belonging to Coke. Hopefully take care of that in the morning and hit the road.
Our crew has disconnected the grease trap in the back room.
It's now sitting in the room, full of grease and other rotten stuff.
The room now smells like what I imagine a gorilla's ass smells like. Someone puts a plastic flower in the protruding pipe, but it doesn't help.

I now have to consciously think about what I'm doing.

A day of heightened activity and too many cans of beer is starting to take its toll!

Lyle got into the beer later in the day, so he's up for some destruction!

These are his last few minutes after 6 or 7 years.

We're both in a strange mood because we've never been in this position before. Save 2 or 3 things, it's a shell now.

No more customers, no more machines.

And 2 drunks in a mall.

I'm kind of mellow, but Lyle starts twisting and breaking light fixtures in the food court.

After 2 or 3 I stop him, as it isn't going to be hard to figure out who did this!

He then throws something into one of the food places.

No real damage. Just a slight mess and they won't notice anyway.

So I beckon Lyle to the washroom area. Here's the Family Washroom.

We'd never been in there ever.

Might as well have a look before we go.

Here's where all our rent money goes!

Look at these nice plush chairs!

I tell Lyle it would probably be a good idea to urinate on them.

Just lift the cushions up, hose the area down, and replace.

Depending on a few variables, these chairs should rot and stink pretty soon.

I assure Lyle of his success with this worthy scientific endeavour.

Only he's a little too eager and coats the chairs!

And he's laughing while he's doing it.

Which means he's urinating everywhere.

And I'm laughing hard as well.

Lyle hits and punches a few more things on the way out of the mall. He's done. He feels great.

I have my styrofoam souvenir.

A couple of things to remove in the morning and I'm free.

A few of us will be driving to California in a few days. Can't wait.

I sleep well. The beer and the demo have me totally unconscious. Six or seven hours of bliss.

I awake with a slight hangover, but more an adrenalin surge as I know the sooner I get this over, the better!

The hood fan guys are coming early, Coke anytime.

The hood fan guys turn out to be the nightmare I knew would come at some point!

Gee, you don't have the proper jacks.

So now they have to go get them.

In the end, they only get half the system down.

They're not smart people at all.

And Coke is nowhere to be seen.

By chance, a Coke Sales Rep is patrolling the mall today.

I don't know her, but I stop her and explain that this stuff has to leave today.

She makes a call or two and then asks me if I can store the equipment for a day or two.

Are you out of your mind?

She then insists I phone the mall and ask about this.

I do it.

I'm stupid.

Who do they put me through to?

I don't even have to tell you.

She's so perky and nice as she tells me all property must be removed by 12 midnight.

I report this to Miss Coke who now pretends none of this happened, and leaves.

The hood fan idiots have only one comment to make

They ask me if I'm going to sleep with Miss Coke or not!

That wasn't exactly the tenure of our conversation, and I remind the wolves of Miss Coke's engagement ring.

Our hopeless romantics tell me that she can remove the ring for a few hours.

THE MALL RAT

I think our little workers have been watching too many movies, and I nod at the still intact hood fan. Idiots.

Getting half of the system out was the best the Stooges could do, and they eventually mumbled some kind of "Gee, we can't do it" line, and disappeared.

They still sent a hefty bill.

So now it's me, 2 Coke machines, and a tin pail filled with ice and beer.

I'm starting to get restless, I'll give Coke another hour or 2, then leave.

Monday commerce is starting to come alive, and I really want no part of it. I just want to leave!

So I tinker with a few things.

With everything out of here, this place is actually very dirty and ugly.

Our painting jobs now look funny, and the stench of the grease trap isn't helping much.

I officially give up on Coke and now have a fountain machine and a cooler to dispose of.

I now trade the cooler, worth about a grand, to a food court neighbour. For "a case of beer."

I thought he'd get me a couple of 24 cases.

He comes back with a six pack and says, "Look, they're imported."

How cheap can you be!!

They're still cheaper than any domestic dozen.

I wonder if he wants the empties back!

Oh well, time to go.

I've been nursing my hangover with lots of beer. Hair of the Dog.

Too many more and I won't be able to turn in the keys.

It's done. Over.

I can't believe it.

From Deepthroat to this moment!

I actually pulled it off.

But the Marketing Lady wins.

I turn the keys in at the Security Office and not the Mall Office.

Time to go.

I walk out the doors.

I'll never enter the food court again.

And the first drops of rain hit my face.
I smile.
Sometimes weather and events coincide.
Nasty weather can turn fine for a funeral. And then turn bad again.
I knew it would rain today, and it's starting now.
It feels good, though.
I'm free.